The Pirate Daughter's Promise

Pirates & Faith – Book One

Molly Evangeline

The Pirate Daughter's Promise

Copyright © 2010 by Molly Evangeline.

www.mollyevangeline.com

Cover Image
© James Steidl | Dreamstime.com

All Scriptures are taken from the New American Standard Bible, Copyright © 1960, 1962, 1963, 1968, 1971, 1972, 1973, 1975, 1977, 1995 by The Lockman Foundation. Used by permission. www.Lockman.org

ISBN 13: 9781450542555
ISBN 10: 1450542557

BOOKS BY MOLLY EVANGELINE

Pirates & Faith Series:
The Pirate Daughter's Promise
Every Tear
A Captain's Heart
Finding Faith

Dedication

To Jesus, my Lord and my Savior, thank you for gifting me with the love and enjoyment I have for writing and thank you for guiding me in every step I've gone through while creating this book.

Mom – Without you, my book would never have made it to this point. I am so thankful to you for teaching me how to write and helping me improve over the years. Thank you.

Sam and Jake – As my younger brothers you've each been a pain at times, but you have always been the first ones I go to with my new story ideas. I've loved fun nights we've stayed up late and read and, Sam, thank you so much for showing me how much you enjoy what I write by always asking if I have more.

Jordyn, Jordan, Dana, and Brandy – You four have been so wonderful in showing your interest and love for my writing. The hours I've spent with each one of you are some of my best memories.

Isaac, Levi, and Jesse – You have shown that my stories can be enjoyed by everyone, not just girls. Your enjoyment of them has thrilled me beyond words. I couldn't ask for cooler cousins.

To the rest of my family, friends, and all of the people who have shown your interest and support in my dream, thank you. It means everything to me.

The Lord also will be a stronghold for the oppressed, a stronghold in times of trouble; and those who know Your name will put their trust in You, for You, O Lord, have not forsaken those who seek You. - Psalms 9:9-10

Prologue

JAMAICA
SUMMER 1702

Daniel McHenry wrapped his calloused hands around the rusted window bars. He could see it through the bars—the gallows. The sinking sun cast the structure's long shadow across the courtyard of the British fort. Two empty nooses swayed in the breeze, waiting. Involuntarily, he touched his throat. He supposed he deserved it after the years spent as a pirate. Yet, that was so long ago. He had been but a boy then. And the thieving he'd done in the last two years had not come at the expense of the innocent. No, he'd robbed pirates in order to return the stolen goods. But that was not enough to erase his past.

Daniel sighed and turned away from the window. Sinking down on the rickety cot in his prison cell, his eyes sought and held those of his first mate in the opposite cell. Caleb was the only one of his crew for which he had not been able to secure an acquittal in regard to the piracy charges. They had been together from the beginning.

A red-coated guard passed between the cells on his routine patrol. He was young, hardly all of twenty. He caught Daniel's gaze but would not hold it. His pale eyes were troubled, Daniel noticed, and his expression unhappy, but he did not say a word.

In time the guard's footsteps died away, and the sound of ocean waves drifted into the cell causing Daniel's heart to yearn for the sea. For all his life it had pulled at him. So many of the events that had shaped his life had taken place at sea.

In these final hours, Daniel had found himself focusing on the significant events of his life—his childhood in a dingy English orphanage, running away, his futile search for his younger brother, and then his arrival in Liverpool where he'd secured his first position on a ship.

It was that event, as a fourteen year old boy, that had put him here now awaiting hanging. It didn't matter that he had redeemed himself in the end. Nor that he was unaware then that he'd signed onto a pirate crew, until it had been too late. Once out at sea, there was no turning back.

He had quickly embraced the adventure of it, though not the bloodthirsty ways of his captain. That was where he and Caleb, another young member of the pirate crew, had found they were alike. It had been their secret dream to leave the infamous Captain Kelley, to find their own ship and become pirate hunters instead of pirates.

Daniel rubbed his forehead with fingers that trembled just a little and reached then into his coat pocket. His fingers closed around two objects there and pulled them out. Tenderly he handled the little leather Bible, worn from many years of use, and the silver-framed portrait that had faded some with time. He couldn't imagine one without the other.

The lovely, young, dark haired woman in the portrait brought a wistful smile to his face. His dear wife, Grace, taken away by sickness at such a young age. But that was one consolation as he neared the end. He would soon see her again, and it was because of her that he had that assurance.

Daniel lifted his head at the clanking echo of the prison door. In a moment there came the sound of heavy footsteps accompanied by the soft padding of smaller feet. He went immediately to the cell door, heart pounding as he waited to lay his eyes on the one and only thing left that made him want to fight his coming fate.

Two guards appeared, walking on either side of a child. Long locks of dark hair framed her small face, just like the woman in his portrait. She was seven years old, and her deep blue eyes were the same shade as his, the color of the ocean on a clear day. His heart ached when he saw the fear in those blue depths of his daughter's eyes.

They stopped at his cell and unlocked the door. As soon as it opened, she rushed into the room, and Daniel caught her up in his arms.

"Skylar." Daniel's voice came out raw with emotion.

He hugged her tightly, noting the soft hair against his cheek and her small arms clinging to his neck. He never wanted to let her go.

Daniel took a seat again on his cot and set his daughter on his knee.

"Are you all right, Skye?" he asked, tucking her hair behind her ears.

3

The little girl nodded, but did not speak. Her wide eyes darted around the dank cell and finally fell on Daniel's face seeking reassurance. Daniel offered her a smile and glanced at the guards who stood stoically beside the closed cell door. He knew this would be the last time he would see Skye before his execution at dawn. This would have to be goodbye, and he didn't know how long the guards would allow his daughter to stay.

"I have some things for you," he said, pulling a thick gold ring set with a marbled red stone from his little finger. From the time she was a toddler, Skye had been fascinated with the ring. "I want you to keep this to always remember me, all right?"

He tucked it into the pocket of the waistcoat she wore. Then he placed Grace's portrait into her hands.

"Mama," Skye murmured, her eyes glued to the likeness.

"Yes, you'll be able to remember both of us. And here is your mother's Bible. Now listen carefully, Skye."

She turned intent eyes back to his face.

"I want you to try to read the Bible every day, just like I taught you, all right?"

Skye nodded dutifully.

"And always remember what Jesus did for you."

Again Skye nodded and sat silent for a long moment. Daniel noticed tears filling her eyes. Her voice trembling, his daughter whispered, "I don't want you to leave me."

Daniel hugged her close and kissed the top of her head, his throat squeezing together. "You're going to have to be brave, Skye, like your mother. Remember the stories I've told you about how brave she was when she was kidnapped by pirates."

"Tell me the story," Skye pleaded.

Daniel glanced at the guards again. They were starting to fidget.

"When your mother was a young woman, she was kidnapped by Captain Kelley. He wanted your grandfather to pay him lots of money to get her back, but when your grandfather did pay him, Kelley wouldn't let her go. He was an evil man and decided to kill her instead. Your mother was very brave. She trusted God and didn't let Kelley scare her. I had never seen anyone so brave," he told her, his voice low and full of wonder. "I fell in love with her while she was Kelley's prisoner and couldn't let him kill her. I helped her out of her cell, and we escaped the ship together.

"When we got to shore, your mother told me all about Jesus' sacrifice on the cross. I believed and was saved."

"Just like me," Skye said.

Daniel smiled. "Yes, just like you. And after I brought your mother back home, God made it so that no one knew I was a pirate. Your mother and I got married and soon after that, God gave us a wonderful gift. You."

A little smile came to Skye's face, warming Daniel's heart. How deeply he wished the story wasn't marked by so much tragedy. Skye had only known her mother for five short years. Then Daniel's past had come to light, forcing him to escape to the sea again, bringing Skye along with him. In his heart he had known it would eventually come to this, and that he'd be caught and held accountable for his crimes. He only wished his daughter would have had a chance to grow older before losing her remaining parent.

"Remember, Skye, I'm your father here on earth, but God is your heavenly Father. He won't ever have to leave you."

One of the guards interrupted. "It's time to finish up."

Daniel stood Skye in front of him and cupped his hands around her small shoulders. He lowered his voice. "Listen carefully, Skye. You remember where we hid our treasure, don't you?"

The treasure he and Caleb had amassed and hidden over the last two years—rewards for the return of pirated goods—was more than enough to make sure Skye would be very well taken care of as an adult.

"Yes, Father."

"You must keep it a secret, all right? Don't tell anyone where it is unless you love them and trust them completely. Will you do that for me?"

Skye looked at him very seriously. "Yes, Father. I promise."

"Good girl." Daniel pulled her into his arms, stroking her hair as she laid her head on his shoulder. "I love you so much, Skye."

She squeezed her arms tighter around his neck. "I love you."

It was like tearing out his heart for Daniel to set her down. "It's time for you to go. You need to say goodbye to Caleb."

The tears in her eyes spilled over onto her cheeks. "I don't want to say goodbye," she cried, eyes flashing with panic. "I don't want to go."

Daniel struggled to keep his own emotions in check, swallowing hard. "I know, sweetheart. But you have to."

He guided her over to the cell door where the guards let her out. Crying softly, she walked over to Caleb's cell. The man knelt at the bars and reached through to put his hand on her shoulder.

"You're a brave girl, Skye, just like your mother," Caleb told her. "Remember everything your father told you. Goodbye, little one."

"Bye," she choked. She then turned and hurried back to her father's cell, bursting into fresh tears.

One of the guards tried to coax her along. "Come on, lass, time to go."

"No!" Skye cried. She grabbed her father's hands. "Please, Father, I don't want to go. *Do something.*"

Daniel's voice broke, his very heart ripping to shreds. "I can't, Skye."

The guards tried to pull her away, but she wouldn't let go. Finally, one of them simply picked her up, and they walked off.

Skye struggled against him frantically, sobbing. "No! Let me go!"

Daniel could hardly bear it. "You won't ever be alone, Skye," he called after them, face pressed between the bars. "God will always be with you. I love you."

They disappeared around the corner, but the sound of his daughter's agonized cries echoed hauntingly until the prison door slammed. When all that was left was silence, Daniel turned away, dragging in a ragged breath. He lifted his face to God, eyes full of pain, as tears rolled down his face.

It had been his mistake to choose the path of a pirate, but God had to have some plan in allowing the secret of his past to come to light, some reason his daughter would face the world without him. Yet, knowing she would suffer because of his actions was almost more than he could stand.

"Oh, Lord, please take care of her."

Chapter One

F umbling in the darkness, Skye tried to pin the front of her dress. Her need for haste and the threadbare material made the task difficult. The worn fabric no longer held the pins securely, reminding her again of the need for a new dress. However, buying material would take so much away from the meager wages she had saved. If only she had even a fraction of the fortune her father had left her. But there might as well be no fortune since she had no one she trusted with the means to take her too it.

"Finally," she whispered when she had the last pin secure. She brushed her hands down her petticoats in an attempt to smooth the wrinkles though many remained.

Although the sun had not yet risen, Skye stepped in front of the mirror hanging on the wall near her bed and hurried to brush her waist-length, nearly black hair. She had to bend just a little to see her dim reflection, making the inheritance of her father's height evident.

After securely pinning up her hair, Skye turned from the mirror, taking a brief moment to look wistfully out

8

the small window above her bed. Out across the stretches of the city and the slowly-lifting fog, she could just make out the sea, gray and vast. Staring at it, she longed for the life she'd lived with her father.

Before going about her business for the day, her gaze fell, landing on her bed where her mother's Bible lay. She grabbed it and knelt down to return it to its hiding place beneath one of the boards under the bed where the young children could not find it and damage it. Rising, she stepped quietly out from behind the patched curtain that separated her from the rest of the huge room. In the dim light, she heard the gentle rise and fall of sleeping children breathing as she walked between two long rows of little beds perpendicular from the walls.

Skye could barely remember what it was like to have her own place to sleep. She had slept in this room with all of the other children for most of her childhood, and after she was old enough to have a job at the orphanage, she had been forced to sleep in the corner to care for any who might wake during the night.

Skye tiptoed out of the room and hurried downstairs. She prayed silently along the way that she would not find herself lectured again for rising too late by Mr. Phillips, the head of the orphanage. With frequent errands to be done in the morning, he expected her to be up early to see to them.

Down in the kitchen, Mr. Phillips was indeed waiting, just as she'd expected. She was spared a lecture, but his pinched face and cold eyes told her she'd only just escaped.

"We need bread for breakfast," he said in a hard voice that Skye had never known to soften. He handed her a large basket and some money, just enough to buy the barest amount and still feed all the children.

"Yes, sir," she said, taking the basket.

Skye left the kitchen smiling a little to herself. Of all her chores, going out to the bakery was one she actually enjoyed. It would take her right past the tailor's shop where her closest friend in the world worked. If she hurried, she would have just enough time to stop there before the shop opened and before he would be busy working for strict Mr. Cunnings all day.

Skye opened the orphanage door and stepped out into the cool, early summer air, causing momentary chills to run through her body. She breathed in deeply of the freshness and looked around the city that had been her birthplace. It was quiet in the early morning, but it would soon become a busy place once the shops opened for business.

Skye walked out into the street, quickening her pace as she headed directly for the tailor's shop. She passed a variety of wood and plaster buildings along the way. The dirt road beneath her soon gave way to cobblestone and many of the buildings turned into more elaborate brick dwellings.

After traveling a couple blocks, she came to the tailor's shop, a two-story white plaster building. At the door, she knocked hopefully, but prepared herself to be greeted by Mr. Cunnings' stern face. In a short moment, the door-knob turned and the door swung open revealing instead a handsome young man, with tied-back dark hair and brown eyes that always shone with care and joy whenever he saw her.

No one held a deeper place in Skye's heart or knew her like William James. They'd grown up in the orphanage together, sharing many times of both hardship and happiness.

Smiling widely, he greeted, "Good morning, Skye."

"Good morning, Will," she replied with a pretty almost-shy smile.

Will glanced at her basket. "Are you going to the bakery?"

"Yes."

"Good," Will responded. "So am I."

"Really?" Skye was delighted that their errands were the same, giving them much more time together.

Will nodded, his pleasure evident in the sparkle of his eyes. "Mr. Cunnings rose this morning and found we had no bread, so he instructed me to go get some." He stepped out of the shop and closed the door. "I'm sure he wanted me to go immediately, but I stalled to see if you'd come by."

"You didn't have to do that." It worried Skye to think of being the cause of trouble for Will with his employer. He had tried for so many jobs before this one.

"It was all right," Will assured her. "I wanted to."

"How are things for you?" Skye asked as they walked away from the shop. Though it had been only a couple days since she'd been able to see him, it felt longer. "Is your skill improving?"

"No, it's not," Will admitted, a frown replacing his once-cheerful look. "I am not meant to be a tailor . . . I don't want to be a tailor."

"Perhaps a new job will come along soon," Skye said hopefully.

"I don't know how Mr. Cunnings has kept me around this long. He's always complaining about my work." Will sighed. "I wish I could work for Matthew again."

"At least life is better for you now than it was at the orphanage," Skye said, trying to encourage him.

"I don't know about that."

Skye glanced at him. "Why not?"

Will's answer did not come right away. He knew it was because he was not able to see her often anymore. He actually missed the years they'd spent growing up together, especially the times the two of them had spent studying God's Word. Skye had changed his life in an incredible way by leading him to Christ. Not only that, but he missed watching over her and taking care of her. He had been her protector for years against the children and orphanage workers who had treated her so poorly. Now, since he had left, Skye had been on her own, largely caring for herself, and it saddened him that sometimes he couldn't be there when she needed him.

Before Will could attempt to tell her any of this, her voice broke through his thoughts.

"There's my grandfather," Skye murmured, her voice low and full of dread.

Despite the trials she had lived through in her young life, Skye had been blessed with an optimistic outlook, strength of heart, and a confidence that carried her through the long hours of each day. The only thing that had ever truly shaken that confidence was her grandfather and the way he treated her.

Just ahead of them, standing in the courtyard of a large, brick merchant's house, an older gentleman held a small white and brown dog. Everything about him spoke of wealth—his home, expensive clothing, the way he carried himself, and the dog, which had been delivered specially from a kennel in England. It all made Skye want to flee.

As she and Will walked by, Skye risked a glance in her grandfather's direction. He met her glance with a cold stare, and she quickly looked away, ruing the fact that she had chanced a look at all. It bewildered her to think that this hard man was her grandfather. The grandfather who had refused to take her in, refused to save her from having to grow up in an orphanage, all for the simple fact that she was the daughter of a pirate.

Just as they were about to pass the house, the man called out, "Excuse me, Mr. James."

The two of them stopped, and Skye's grandfather strode toward them. Skye sidestepped closer to Will, hoping to shield herself by his presence, yet when her grandfather reached them, she might as well have been invisible to him.

"Mr. James, what a fortunate coincidence," he said with a smile. "I planned to stop by sometime today to ask Mr. Cunnings a question, but I will ask you and save the trip. I would like to have a new waistcoat made of silk. Could you tell me how much it would cost?"

"I'm sorry, Mr. Young," Will said with regret, "but I'm afraid I'm not doing well as a tailor's apprentice. I don't think I could accurately give you a price."

"Just an estimate would be fine," Mr. Young pressed.

"All I can really say is that it would be quite expensive," Will replied finally.

He and Skye tried to go on, but Mr. Young stopped Will again.

"I'm quite impressed with you, Mr. James. You've done well for having come from an orphanage. You have a good job, and with a few of the right friends, you could do very well. If you'd like, I could introduce you to a few very respectable acquaintances."

13

Skye shifted and swallowed hard. She kept her eyes on the cobbled street, afraid that her face would show the sadness welling up inside of her. Obviously, her grand-father did not consider her worthy enough to be called a respectable acquaintance, even for Will who wasn't really any different from her. Both had very low standing in society growing up as orphans. The only real difference between them was Skye's tainted reputation as a pirate's daughter.

Sensing Skye's great discomfort, Will replied quickly, "You do not have to trouble yourself, Mr. Young. I am very thankful for the good friends I have already. Thank you anyway." Not wishing for Mr. Young to say anything more to hurt Skye, he continued, "Now if you'll excuse me, I must be going or Mr. Cunnings will be upset that I took so long."

Mr. Young nodded. "Very well. Good day, Mr. James."

"Good day," Will replied politely and he guided Skye along, away from the house.

When they had gone farther, she murmured, "He ignored me again. Just as he always does. It's as if I don't even exist to him."

Will shook his head, confused. "I can't understand it. He loved your mother, right?"

"More than anything," Skye told him.

"I've heard more people than I can remember say that you look just like her," Will stated. "I can't imagine him not loving you. In a sense, he'd be gaining back what he lost."

Skye shook her head with regret. "All he sees is that I'm the result of his daughter marrying a pirate."

Will looked at her sadly and was quick to change the subject, hoping to distract her from the difficulty with her grandfather. She had enough on her mind without the added sting of being shunned by the only family she had left.

Chapter Two

Another clear day dawned over the Caribbean. After a quick breakfast, Mr. Young left his house early with a mission to order a new waistcoat, the price of little concern. He strode into the tailor's shop and looked around. The walls inside were well stocked with shelves full of brightly-colored bolts of fabric, Mr. Cunnings being one of the few tailors who sold the fabric of the clothes he made. A couple large tables and work areas were set up with sewing supplies and equipment. Across the room, Mr. Young spotted Mr. Cunnings and Will at a long table measuring out a piece of cloth.

Mr. Cunnings looked up and smiled expressively when he noticed Mr. Young enter. Quickly straightening his wig and smoothing his coat, he hurried to meet Mr. Young, his eagerness for the business painfully obvious as he asked, "Good day, sir. What can I do for you?"

"I want a new silk waistcoat," Mr. Young told him. "What would be the cost?"

Mr. Cunnings calculated, considering Mr. Young's size, which was certainly not substantial, and the cost of the materials. "It would come to about forty pounds, but for you, I'll make it thirty."

Nodding, Mr. Young seemed quite pleased with the price and said, "If you can have it done by tomorrow morning in time for a dinner I'm hosting, I'll pay an extra pound."

"It's a deal," Mr. Cunnings replied, a grin stretching wide across his thin face. "We shall have it done. Now, what color would you like?" He gestured conspicuously towards several different-colored bolts of silk.

Mr. Young studied them for a few moments before deciding on a color he liked. Mr. Cunnings quickly took the measurements he needed and Mr. Young was free to go. He thanked Mr. Cunnings, said good day, and left the shop.

Will let a small sigh escape when Mr. Cunnings hastily instructed him to clear the work area. With a deadline to meet, the man would be even more impatient and demanding than usual. The next hours were sure to be unpleasant. Mr. Cunnings spread out the silk they needed on the newly-cleared surface and the two went right to work on the waistcoat.

A knock at the door interrupted Skye on her way to straighten the children's room. With no one else around, she answered it. The mail carrier greeted her in a friendly fashion and gave her a handful of mail for the orphanage. Skye thanked him politely, closed the door, and took the mail straight to Mr. Phillips in his office. He flipped through it as she turned to leave, but he called her back, his forehead wrinkling in a deep frown as he pulled out three of the letters.

"These are addressed to Mr. Young," Mr. Phillips stated. "They must have somehow been mixed in with ours." He turned his stern eyes to Skye, making her flinch slightly. Though she had grown up, it was never far from her mind that this man had raised his hand to her on numerous occasions over the years. "I want you to take them to him at once."

Skye's eyes widened. "Me?"

"Yes."

Mr. Phillips handed Skye the packets. For a moment, Skye only stared at them, her gaze fixed on her grandfather's name.

"Well, what are you waiting for?" Mr. Phillips snapped.

"Nothing," Skye murmured and promptly left the room.

At the front door, she slowed and swallowed hard. How could she go to her grandfather's house and face him, converse with him? The last time she had spoken to him was just a hazy memory, clouded by many years. Yet what choice did she have? Mr. Phillips would never be understanding of her reasons for saying she couldn't do it. His response would be to threaten her with the loss of one of the very few privileges she had or even her job.

Resigning herself to her task, Skye pulled open the door and reluctantly stepped out. The city was noisy and very busy, the opposite of the peaceful early morning she had enjoyed with Will the day before. She walked into the bustling street and headed toward her grandfather's house, dread mounting. Along the way, she glanced in desperation at the tailor's shop, silhouettes of customers appearing through the window. She knew Will must be busy, but she longed to see him walk out of the shop and take the letters for her. However, the door remained closed as she passed by.

Skye hesitated when she came to the entrance of her grandfather's courtyard. Her eyes followed the cobblestone walkway leading up to the large front door of the huge brick house. The brilliant green lawn and beautifully-tended flower gardens made her feel entirely out of place, but she made herself keep walking and tried to calm her nerves.

Stopping at the top step in front of the door, Skye silently asked God to help her and give her strength. She took a deep breath and knocked cautiously. It startled her when the door opened almost as soon as she had taken her hand away.

Her grandfather stood in the doorway, hat tucked neatly under his arm, apparently on his way out. When he realized who had come to call, his eyes narrowed in an irritated manner.

"What is it?" he asked brusquely.

Skye licked her lips and her voice wavered a little as she explained, "Your mail somehow got mixed in with that of the orphanage. I was sent to give it to you."

She held out the packet of letters and her grandfather took them. He flipped through the stack with a frown before he settled an accusing gaze on his granddaughter.

"You didn't lose or keep any of it, did you?"

Skye's heart plummeted. Did her grandfather really think her a thief just because she was the daughter of a former pirate?

"N-no, I didn't," Skye stammered.

Mistrust colored her grandfather's expression as he closed the door without so much as a simple word of thanks. But just before it closed completely, she heard, "I find that difficult to believe."

Skye stared at the door for long miserable seconds before backing down the steps. Slowly, she walked out of the courtyard beset by terrible dejection. She made a determined effort to fight back the tears pooling in her eyes. Skye rarely allowed herself to cry, only silently in bed at night, but soon she could hold them back no longer and they trickled down her face. She walked down the street, head bowed, her grandfather's words replaying in her mind. Every time they repeated, they stung deeper.

But something shattered the echo of the words. Her name was called. Looking up, she filled with relief. Will hurried to her.

"Skye, what's wrong?" he asked, worried at seeing her tears.

Skye wiped them away as she told Will what had taken place at her grandfather's, pouring out all the sorrow that had built. She tried to prevent more tears from falling, but it was useless. The cry helped her feel better, but nothing could erase the sting of what her grandfather had said.

"I just long for a family to love and take care of me," Skye told him miserably as she wiped her wet cheeks. "Sometimes I can't stand how badly I miss my father."

Will laid his hands comfortingly on her shoulders. "I know you know this better than anyone, but don't forget that God is also your Father, and He loves and cares for you constantly," he reminded gently. "He has a plan. This may not comfort you, but what would have happened to me if you had not come to the orphanage? I might never have known Christ."

Skye looked up at him, a smile finally coming to her face. "You're right. And yes, it does comfort me. You are my dearest friend, Will. Thank you."

Will smiled and silence followed for a moment before Skye spoke again.

"I must get back to the orphanage. I have so much to do. If I don't get back at it, I won't get it done. Mr. Phillips has already threatened to throw me out once this week. Although I don't believe he's serious, I'd better not risk it."

"I'm sorry I held you up," Will said, truly worried for her.

Skye shook her head. "Don't be. I would still feel terrible right now if I had not talked to you. I needed it."

"I'm thankful that I was here to help you. Now I don't want to keep you any longer," Will urged her gently. "Maybe we'll see each other tomorrow."

"And in church on Sunday," Skye said. "I'll pray that I can come."

"I will too," Will promised. "And I will pray about your grandfather."

"Thank you," Skye told him with a smile.

And with that, they parted. Will remained where he stood as he watched Skye disappear down the street, and only then did he continue on his way back to the shop. It still worried him to think that Skye could be sent away from the orphanage. But if that did happen, he would use every shilling of his wages to make sure she had a good place to stay.

Will's mind turned then to what he had told Skye. *God isn't the only one who loves and cares about her*, he thought. *How do I tell her that?* He could never seem to find the right words or the right time.

Skye met Mr. Phillips as soon as she came through the front door. By the scowl on his face, she knew that he was not happy, and she braced herself for whatever harsh words might follow.

"What took you so long?" he demanded.

Skye was slow to speak, knowing he'd be upset with her answer. "I met Will on the way back," she told him meekly.

Mr. Phillips' eyes narrowed. "Haven't I warned you not to waste your time talking to people when you go out?"

"Please, Mr. Phillips, I hardly get to see Will since he left," Skye tried to explain.

"That's what your days off are for," he snapped. "And today isn't one of them. If you waste any more time, you definitely will not be attending church on Sunday."

Skye stayed silent and went back to her work, determined not to do anything that would jeopardize her privilege to attend church. From past experience, she knew that Mr. Phillips didn't care how important it was to her and that he needed very little provoking to forbid her to go.

The rest of the day passed with a shadow over it, but Skye found great comfort in the passages of her Bible when she'd been allowed to go to her bed for the night. The words of 2 Corinthians 1:3-4 brought a smile to her face. *Blessed be the God and Father of our Lord Jesus Christ, the Father of mercies and God of all comfort, who comforts us in all our affliction so that we will be able to comfort those who are in any affliction with the comfort with which we ourselves are comforted by God.*

Chapter Three

Will was careful not to let even a speck of dust from the street reach Mr. Young's new waistcoat. He did not want any reason for the man to be displeased after he had worked on it late into the night, enduring Mr. Cunnings' harsh criticism and complaints. The tailor had said that if Will were better at tailoring, the waistcoat wouldn't have taken so long. *I need to find a new job*, Will thought. Mr. Cunnings wasn't the only one getting frustrated.

At the front door of the merchant house, Will paused, thinking for a moment how poor Skye must have felt standing here. With a sigh, he knocked and the housekeeper let him into the large, well-furnished foyer.

"I will tell Mr. Young that you are here," the prim woman said as she walked into another room.

Will let his eyes scan the room as he waited. Just the foyer alone was as large as the tailor's shop workroom. Masterpieces of artwork, which must have cost a fortune, hung on the walls. If the foyer was decorated in such a way, what must the rest of the house be like? Will couldn't even imagine what it would be like to live like this.

Shortly, Mr. Young entered the room and appeared to be very pleased by the sight of the new waistcoat.

"Good day, Mr. James. The waistcoat looks excellent," Mr. Young praised.

"The credit goes to Mr. Cunnings. He made it and the most I did was to irritate him with how little I have learned about being a tailor," Will admitted.

"Nonsense," Mr. Young replied good-naturedly. "I am sure you've learned a great deal."

"Really, I haven't," Will insisted, modestly. "I'm hoping to find a new job as soon as I can."

"Well, if you need any help finding one, I'd be happy to assist you," Mr. Young offered.

"Thank you, Mr. Young, I'll keep that in mind," Will told him.

"Good."

A brief pause hung between them until Will spoke hesitantly. "Before I leave, Mr. Young, may I ask you a question?"

"Of course," Mr. Young answered generously.

Will hesitated again and finally asked, "Why is it that you despise your granddaughter?"

Mr. Young's expression changed instantly. He stared hard at Will. "And why should the way I feel about the girl be any concern of yours?" He refused to acknowledge that Skye was his granddaughter.

"Because I care a great deal about her," Will answered.

"Well, perhaps you should find someone else to place at the center of your affections," Mr. Young said shortly. "Someone without such a reputation. You might find that you'd be offered more opportunities."

Will stood in shock over the response. "I would never turn my back on Skye. I don't care what people think of me for being her friend and taking care of her," he declared. "To me, no opportunity could be worth losing her."

Clearly uncomfortable, Mr. Young's voice came out harsher than usual. "Young man, I really don't see that I have any obligation to discuss this with you."

"Please, Mr. Young," Will pressed. "I only want to understand."

"She is a reminder that my beautiful daughter married a liar and a thief," Mr. Young said bitterly. "I can only expect that Miss McHenry is of that nature as well."

Will shook his head, his protectiveness kicking in on high. "Then you would be mistaken. Skye has never stolen or lied about anything in the eleven years I've known her. She is an honest, good person who has been living a horrible, lonely life. You may not realize that in the orphanage she has been cruelly ridiculed and rejected by everyone, not just the other children. She is being treated as a servant, having to get up early every morning and work late into the night. She is at the beck and call of the orphanage because no one else will even consider hiring her. Even as a child, she was forced to work for them. It is the only way she can survive and even there she is in danger of being thrown out." He paused and then said with feeling, "All she wants is a family to love her."

"How do you know this for sure?" Mr. Young asked.

"Because I've seen it and though I have never once heard her complain, she often tells me how much she wants to be accepted and loved. I am one of the few who will listen to her," Will answered. "I met her yesterday just after she brought you your mail, and she was in tears because of what you said about—"

"Mr. James," Mr. Young interrupted. "I will not stand here and argue with you over something I would much rather not discuss."

Will stood quietly in the awkward silence. Arguing had not been his intention. All he had wanted was to try to help Skye, but he knew he was getting nowhere and might possibly have made things worse.

"I'm sorry I brought it up," he said finally.

Will handed the waistcoat to Mr. Young, who, in turn, gave him payment for it. Saying a quiet good day, Will left the house, defeated. He really had hoped for his discussion with Mr. Young to turn out better.

Skye scanned Mr. Phillips' list and searched the shop shelves. A couple of the items were needed for the evening meal so she had to hurry. Just as she finished collecting everything, she glanced up at the sound of the little bell on the door. The intimidating form of her grandfather walked into the shop. Skye's heart skipped in panic. How could she face him after their encounter yesterday? She spun around so he wouldn't catch her staring at him.

Skye stood for a long moment, trying to decide what to do. Taking a deep breath, she finally carried her items up to the counter. She shouldn't have waited. Her grandfather came up behind her with his items only a moment later. Skye stood rigidly, trying to hide the fact that she was nearly shaking inside. The clerk added up her total while she mentally begged him to hurry. She tried to swallow, but her mouth was too dry. She could almost feel her grandfather's critical gaze boring into her back.

At last the clerk finished and Skye took a handful of coins from her pocket. She counted out the amount, thanking God that she was able with her frazzled mind. Skye gathered up her purchases, nearly more than she could carry, and fled the shop.

Pricked with a feeling of reluctant curiosity, Mr. Young found himself turning to watch his granddaughter leave. On her way out, he happened to see a small package slip out of her grasp. When he saw that she didn't realize she had dropped it, he was dismayed. He knew a gentleman would return it to her, but this was not something he had any desire to do.

Skye tried to shift her packages ever so slightly. Mr. Phillips would be furious if she lost something. Now she wished she had thought to bring a basket. *Please, Lord, don't let me drop anything.*

She had gone less than a block when an unexpected voice came from behind her.

"Miss McHenry."

Skye stopped, nervousness gripping her again. She turned slowly to face her grandfather. Her eyes went first to his face, but they quickly dropped to the package he held. She recognized it as one of her parcels and the very thing the orphanage needed for supper.

"You dropped this on your way out," Mr. Young informed her in a voice that held no feeling whatsoever.

"Thank you, sir," Skye replied shyly but politely, as she shifted what she was carrying enough to take the package. "I didn't even notice."

Silence. Skye's heart beat hard.

"Have you always been sent on errands like this?" Mr. Young questioned. His voice was no longer as stern and cold.

Skye blinked in surprise. The last time he'd spoken to her in a civil manner had been when she was a small child.

"Yes, sir," Skye answered. "Either that or one of the maids, but it's mainly me."

"None of the children?" Mr. Young asked.

"No, sir," Skye answered truthfully. "But that is what I'm paid for."

Her grandfather nodded tersely. "Well, good day, Miss McHenry."

"Good day," Skye replied, her words trailing off into a stunned silence as she watched him walk away. She could hardly believe what had happened as she turned to walk back to the orphanage. It was the first time since she'd been orphaned that her grandfather had not ignored her or treated her with disdain.

The wondering of it nearly caused her to bump right into Will.

"Sorry, Will," she apologized quickly. "I guess I wasn't paying attention to where I was going."

"That's all right," Will assured her with a smile and made certain that she hadn't dropped anything. Curious over her distraction, he said, "You seem to have a lot on your mind."

"Well, it's the strangest thing. I was just at one of the shops. My grandfather came in while I was there. On the way out, I dropped something without realizing it, and he returned it to me. Not only did he do that, but he asked me a few questions and almost treated me kindly," Skye said, still bewildered.

Will smiled. Maybe it had done good to confront Mr. Young about his behavior toward Skye. "Perhaps things are changing."

"I hope so," Skye replied, though she didn't want to get her hopes up too high. Then, remembering what Mr. Phillips had told her the day before, she said, "I'm sorry I can't talk to you more, Will, but I must get back. Supper is about to be started, and if I'm late I won't be able to attend church."

"I understand," Will said. "If I could, I'd help you carry your things, but I don't suppose Mr. Phillips or Mr. Cunnings would take kindly to that."

Skye shook her head with regret. "No, I don't think so."

They parted with reluctant goodbyes, and Skye hurried back.

That night in bed, after she had prayed and read her Bible, Skye's thoughts once again settled on her grandfather. What had caused the change of attitude towards her? Would anything else come of it? Skye asked herself these questions as she slowly drifted off to sleep.

Chapter Four

D awn had not yet arrived when Skye sat up straight in bed. Something had disturbed her sleep, but it was not the normal cry of one of the children. A loud rumble like distant thunder came from outside. She rose to look out her window. Toward the bay, orange flashes of light erupted in the fog, followed by more rumbling. *Cannons.* Her mind recognized the sound immediately from her days of sailing.

Skye grabbed her dress and put it on as quickly as she could. If cannons were firing, the city was under attack. Securing the last pin, Skye heard a tremendous crash downstairs. Thankful that all the children remained sleeping, she hurried from the room and down the hall, praying that whatever was happening, God would protect the city.

When she came to the stairs and peered down into the foyer below, Skye saw the orphanage door splintered. All that was left was a gaping hole. Several rough men stood inside, some holding torches, and one had Mr. Phillips by the collar of his nightclothes. Skye had no doubt they were pirates and couldn't imagine their reason for wanting to attack an orphanage of all places. The pirate was demanding something of Mr. Phillips though she could not hear what it was, when all of a sudden several pirates started for the stairs.

Skye pressed herself against the wall, hoping they had not seen her. Her first thoughts were for the children, especially the youngest ones, and how frightened they'd be. It made her forget any fear that she may have had for herself. Determined not to let the pirates reach their rooms, she took hold of a chair that stood beside her and waited, heart pounding.

Right as the first two pirates reached the top of the stairs, Skye swung the chair around and hit them hard. Completely unsuspecting, they tumbled backwards, taking many of the others down with them. After recovering, they tried again. Skye held them back for a moment, but one of the pirates caught hold of her arm and yanked the chair from her hands. She fought desperately to get away, but a second pirate grabbed her other arm and they dragged her down the stairs.

At the bottom, they jerked her to a stop in front of the pirate who had been speaking to Mr. Phillips who now cowered against the wall. The pirate grabbed Skye's wrist and yanked her close to peer at the ring on her index finger, the ring her father had given her. He nodded in satisfaction to the others and the fearsome group carried her along out of the orphanage. She struggled as hard as she could to get away, but she was no match for their strength as they dragged her through the dark and deserted city streets.

Skye's efforts exhausted her by the time they arrived at the beach. She looked out into the bay and caught sight of a large, dark galleon. The pirates bound her hands tightly behind her back and made her climb into a longboat waiting on shore.

A deafening boom exploded followed by a crash. Skye looked in the direction of the fort, which stood near the edge of the bay. Flames leapt from the structure and lit up the sky. It seemed that the soldiers there could do nothing against their attackers, for no shots were fired in return. The pirates rowed the longboat with great speed toward their ship.

At the galleon, the men on deck hoisted the longboat up and Skye was forced to board. Pirates scurried around preparing to escape port before the navy ships could be sent after them. Glancing up at the sails, Skye spotted a very large flag fluttering ominously from the mainmast. She shuddered. The flag was red, a sign of no mercy.

The pirates leading Skye came to a sudden halt. A man stood before them, tall and dressed in dark clothes, wearing a big, black, three-cornered hat. In the darkness, Skye could not make out his face, but she could tell that he was grinning evilly.

"Take 'er below," he commanded in a low, grating voice as he turned away.

Before she could speak a word of protest, the pirates forced Skye down one of the hatchways and through several stale, dark passageways below deck. Finally, they came to a group of small, iron-barred cells. They shoved her into one and quickly locked it. Standing uncertainly at the door, she watched the pirates leave.

Alone, Skye took in what little she could see of her surroundings, unable to comprehend what had happened or what the pirates intended to do with her. Clearly no one else had been taken captive, and she had seen no loot being brought aboard, which meant only one thing—she was what they had been after. A deep dread settled over her.

Weary from her struggles, Skye backed farther into the cell and sat down with a slight shudder on the damp wooden floor. Waves rushed against the sides as they sailed, the ship's timbers creaked, and men shouted on deck. Darkness surrounded her. At the orphanage, Skye had not had time to worry, but now a sense of fear crept through her body. Why had she been kidnapped and what did the pirates intend to do with her?

After more than an hour had passed, Skye found a sparkle of light as sunshine streamed through a thin crack in the ship's side. It gave her a tiny boost of confidence, but then heavy footsteps approached. She rose quickly as two filthy pirates came to her cell. Without a word, they unlocked it and walked inside. Grabbing her arms, they pulled her out and took her above deck. Emerging into the sunlight, Skye squinted, her gaze darting around the ship. Many pirates worked on deck and glared at her cruelly as she was dragged past them.

The pirate captors brought Skye into the large, richly-furnished captain's cabin. At a table in the center of the expansive space sat the man Skye had seen earlier. She studied him now in the light of day and figured him to be in his late fifties with long, dark hair that was dyed to keep the graying areas hidden. He had it pulled back, and his beard and mustache were short, neatly kept, and also dyed. His dark clothes were quite fine and decorated in part with intricate embroidery. The belts he wore had expertly-crafted silver buckles, and Skye got the impression that he was a man who cared a great deal about his appearance, unlike most of the crew.

The man studied her closely in return, until he nodded slowly to the pirates. One of them yanked out a large dagger. Skye braced herself, but the pirate merely cut the ropes from her wrists. With that, they left the cabin, closing the doors behind them. Skye glanced down at her reddened wrists and rubbed them before looking up again as the man spoke.

"I am Francis, the captain of this ship. Welcome aboard, Miss . . ."

The condescending tone of the captain's voice made Skye dislike him immediately. He wanted her name, but she refused to say anything.

"Very well, may I ask the names of your parents? Or don't you know?" he suggested unkindly, determined to get an answer one way or another.

Skye hesitated for a moment. "I don't think I want to answer that."

Francis peered at her suspiciously. "Why not?"

"You're a pirate, why would I?"

"You're so confident that's what we are. Obviously you must be familiar with pirates."

He was trying to trap her. Skye was sure of it. "I saw your flag," she stated matter-of-factly, neither denying nor admitting to his statement.

"I see," Francis murmured. "Tell me, have you ever heard of Daniel McHenry?"

Skye's heart took a hard stumble at the mention of her father's name, and she answered tentatively, "Yes."

"How?"

"Everyone has heard stories about him." Skye knew she was not lying. Her father's exploits as a pirate hunter had been known far and wide. Growing up, she had heard countless stories about him.

"I would not lie to me if I were you, girl," he warned. "That ring you have on is unique. There is only

34

one man who had it and that was Daniel McHenry. The only person he would have given it to before he died would have been his daughter Skylar. Not only does that prove you are her, but you bear a stunning resemblance to both your parents, your mother particularly. Now you'd better start answering my questions honestly or you'll be terribly sorry. Your father was Daniel McHenry, wasn't he?"

Skye stared at Francis for a few seconds, processing his words. How did he know so much?

"Fine," she confessed. "My father was Daniel McHenry. How is it you knew my parents?"

Francis smiled victoriously. "I only told you my first name. Does Captain Francis *Kelley* sound familiar?"

Skye took a step back at the shock of it. "You're the pirate my father sailed for until you kidnapped my mother!"

"That's right, I—"

"What is it you want?" Skye asked, not waiting for Kelley to finish.

Kelley's grin widened. "Well, Miss McHenry, I would like to discuss the location of your father's treasure."

Everything became frighteningly clear and dread pulsed through Skye. Kelley had kidnapped her specifically to learn the location of the treasure. The treasure she had promised her father she would never give up the location to.

"What about it?" Skye asked cautiously.

"Where is it?" Kelley demanded.

"What makes you think I know?"

Kelley slammed his fist on the table, causing Skye to jump slightly. He had expected to quickly learn everything he'd wanted to know. He hadn't planned on Skye opposing him. *What did you expect from the daughter of someone like old McHenry?* Kelley scowled.

"You are his daughter."

"I was only seven years old when he died," Skye reminded him.

"And I've heard stories that you were almost as good a navigator as he was. Now are those stories true or were you a worthless little girl who knew nothing?"

Skye didn't know how to answer, but her silence told Kelley everything he wanted to know.

Kelley leered over his table and spoke slowly, taking time with every word. "Where is the treasure?"

A determined fire lit inside Skye and she answered simply, but boldly, "I will never tell you."

Kelley glared at her. "Under the circumstances, I hardly see that as a wise choice."

"I promised my father the day he died that I would tell no one."

"No one?" Kelley asked slowly.

"Unless it is someone I love and trust completely."

"Have you told anyone yet?"

"No," Skye admitted.

"Is there anyone you've thought of telling?" Kelley coaxed with a smirk.

Skye did not answer.

"Who is it?"

"I don't see it as a wise decision to tell you," Skye answered, thinking only of Will and his safety.

"You may think you're wise, but the wise thing to do now would be to tell me where that treasure is," Kelley's voice lowered threateningly, "and save yourself a whole lot of *discomfort*."

"I will not tell you anything," Skye declared, unmoved by the threat.

Kelley's eyes narrowed cruelly. "Well, I'm sure that after you get a taste of my means of persuasion, you'll see that I'm serious."

"And you'll see that I'm serious," Skye shot back.

"Brave comment, girl, but still not a wise one," Kelley warned.

Short on patience, he called the other two pirates back into the cabin. Kelley nodded and they took Skye by the arms.

"Take 'er back to 'er cell," Kelley commanded them irritably.

Chapter Five

Will rushed down the street as the rising sun crept over the city. The cannon blasts had sounded nearly an hour ago, but until the sun had risen, Mr. Cunnings had refused to let him leave the shop. People crowded his way as they talked noisily amongst themselves about what had happened, but he did not pause. He had only one goal on his mind.

Finally, Will broke from the crowd and arrived in front of the orphanage. He skid to a halt and his heart nearly stopped. The orphanage door lay in pieces and several red-coated soldiers patrolled the area. Two stood guard at the entrance. Will hurried up to them, desperate to find Skye.

"No one is allowed inside," one of the soldiers said, hastily blocking him from entering.

Fear tinged Will's voice. "What happened?"

Thinking Will was just another one of the many people who had already asked the same question, the second soldier told him, "We are not giving any information."

"But I—"

"I'm sorry, sir," the guard interrupted, "but information will be given to citizens of the city by Lieutenant Avery as soon as possible

Will stared at the guard for a moment and then looked past him into the orphanage, hoping to catch some glimpse of Skye, to assure himself that she was safe. Finally, knowing he wouldn't learn what he wanted from the soldiers and might wait all day watching for Skye, he headed to the fort.

He had to find Lieutenant Avery. It was Will's hope that the man would take time to answer his questions. Will believed he would. They had met on several occasions in the past, and Avery had always been very friendly toward him.

When Will reached the badly-damaged fort, he spotted Avery amongst the soldiers and worked his way over to him.

"Lieutenant Avery," Will called.

Avery turned to him, his face grave. Will only briefly took in the sheer damage done to the fort before asking, "What happened?"

"I have been asked that question numerous times already today, and like I've told everyone, the people will be addressed as soon as possible," Avery answered.

"I understand that," Will said respectfully, knowing the lieutenant must be weary. "But please, I must know what happened."

Avery sighed and then gave in. "As you can see, pirates attacked this morning not long before dawn and blew up most of the fort and homes around it. They didn't loot any part of the city, but they took a girl from the orphanage."

"Who?" Will asked. Dread churned his stomach.

"That girl who works there—Daniel McHenry's daughter."

Heart sinking, Will cast his eyes out to sea. "Skye," he murmured in dismay. Looking back at Avery, he said, "What is being done to rescue her?"

Avery hesitated. "I remember now you were friends with the girl so that makes it difficult to say this, but I don't think trying to rescue her is necessary. We don't believe that the pirates kidnapped her, but, in fact, helped her get out of the orphanage."

"No, I know that is not true," Will said with absolute certainty. "The only ones she knew before she was put in the orphanage were the men from her father's crew and they would never have done all this damage. Not to mention, *she* would never do anything like this or leave without telling me first."

"I'm sorry, but without specific evidence of that, we cannot take the time to go after her right now," Avery told him. "The damage to the fort must be repaired in case of another attack."

Will shook his head. "Or maybe it is because she's an orphan and not important enough to rescue?"

"That's not what I'm saying," Avery insisted.

But Will did not believe it. "If she were the daughter of one of the wealthy families in this city, you would be out searching for her this very minute."

Avery opened his mouth to speak, but said nothing for a long moment. "I truly am sorry I can't help you," he told Will flatly. "I would like to, but that is not my call. Right now, we must do what's best for the city."

He was about to walk away, but Will stopped him.

"Can you at least tell me anything about the pirates or the ship?" Will pled.

Avery sighed. "From various reports, we believe that the ship is the *Finder*, which is captained by a pirate named Francis Kelley. That's all I can tell you."

He turned to leave but Will stopped him once more.

"You said his name is Kelley?"

"Yes."

"I have heard that name before," Will murmured to himself.

"Not surprising. He is said to have been one of the most feared pirates around, though it has been some years since he's done anything like this," Avery said as he walked away.

Will watched him go. What could he do now? No question, Skye had to be rescued. The question was, how? He turned and hurried back into the city. Only one other person he knew could help him.

As Will pushed his way through the crowded streets once more, he suddenly came to a stop. He remembered where he had heard the name Kelley before. Skye had mentioned it. Captain Kelley was the one Skye's father had sailed for when he was a pirate. And he was the one who had kidnapped Skye's mother.

But that wasn't the worst of it. Skye had told him about her father's hidden treasure and her promise to him. *Kelley is after the treasure,* Will realized. Skye would never tell him where the treasure was even if her life depended on it. Will knew this for sure, and a man like Kelley would stop at nothing to find it.

Skye was sitting against the wall in prayer when footsteps approached her cell again. This time it sounded like only one person and the footsteps weren't as loud and heavy as the ones before. Skye looked up as lantern light flickered into the cabin, surprised to find the pirate was actually a woman. She had long, black hair and dark skin, an ex-slave most likely, or perhaps still one. She wore a stained white shirt, a pair of dark breeches, and a dark blue sash.

"Captain says to enjoy this. It'll be all ya eat 'til ya tell 'im where that treasure is," the woman informed her.

Until then, Skye had not realized the woman held a plate of food in her hands. She unlocked the cell and opened it just wide enough to hand Skye the cold, metal plate. Skye stood up and took it slowly. She walked closer to the cell bars as the woman relocked the door.

"Tell the captain that if he starves me to death, the location of the treasure will go with me," Skye said, wanting Kelley to know that one threat wasn't enough to intimidate her.

The woman seemed surprised by her bold words, and then turned to walk away. However, Skye, still curious about seeing a woman pirate, spoke before she could leave.

"What is your name?"

The woman paused as if debating whether or not to answer. She glanced over her shoulder. "Kate."

When she was gone, Skye turned her eyes to the plate of food. It couldn't really be called a meal. A small tin cup of water balanced on the place next to a piece of hardtack and a piece of dried meat which Skye decided against eating. That was all. She nibbled on the hardtack and sipped the water. It tasted as though it had been sitting in a barrel for far too long. After that, she ate no more having no appetite.

Skye sat again and found her thoughts turning to Will. What was going on back in Kingston? Did Will know yet that she had been kidnapped? If he did, what was he doing? She knew he would be worried sick and wondered if anyone would do anything to rescue her. The more she thought about it, the more unlikely it seemed. No one in Kingston would waste time going after an orphaned pirate's daughter. No one but Will. Yet how could he rescue her without help? It was impossible.

Will took a quick glance at the familiar, worn sign hanging above the door. It read, *Cabinetry and Blacksmith* and brought back memories. This had been his first job before going to work for Mr. Cunnings a couple of months ago. How he longed to have this job back.

Dismissing his memories, Will knocked earnestly on the door, which was still closed because of the early hour. He shifted anxiously, waiting for it to open. In a moment, a tall man appeared, his years measuring late thirties and a leather blacksmith apron covered the front of his plain, tradesman clothes. His dark brown hair hung level with his shoulders and ocean blue eyes sparkled with happiness as a smile spread across his face. However, when he noticed Will's worried expression, the smile quickly vanished.

"What's wrong, Will?" he asked.

"Have you heard about the pirates?"

"Yes, I offered help to Lieutenant Avery, but he didn't have anything for me to do so I came back here."

"Matthew, they've kidnapped Skye."

Matthew's face paled. "Are you certain?"

43

"Avery told me himself."

"Is he doing anything to rescue her?"

"No, and she is in terrible trouble if someone doesn't help her. It's Captain Kelley who's taken her, the one Skye's father sailed with. He's after Skye's treasure, I'm sure of it." Filled with distress, Will stated further, "I know Skye will never tell him the location of it and who knows what Kelley will do to her when she doesn't."

Matthew nodded as he took in the information. "Go quickly and tell Mr. Cunnings you're leaving. Get whatever you need. Meet me at the docks in ten minutes. We need to find a ship and a crew to go after Kelley."

Matthew closed the door as soon as Will was gone and went to his weapon cabinet. Wiping his soot-covered hands hastily on his apron, he opened the cabinet doors. A row of swords, all made by him, lined the inside.

But he wasn't just a blacksmith. He was a carpenter as well, his furniture some of the best in Kingston, yet despite that fact, he barely made enough money to keep the business going. That was the reason he had wanted Will to find a better job. There had not been enough money for both of them to live on. It was also one reason he had never been able to adopt Skye as he had long wanted to do. And now she was in the hands of bloodthirsty pirates. Fear for her life settled in his heart.

Matthew had known Skye and Will for about six years now. Ever since they'd met in church. They were like the daughter and son he'd never had.

Taking a sword out of the cabinet, Matthew laid it on a bench and pulled off his apron. Going into the bedroom of his small house, he packed some extra clothes and his Bible into a duffel. After making sure his furnace had burned down, he walked out of the shop, locked the door, and headed for the docks.

Will came in the door so fast he obviously startled Mr. Cunnings who stood at the counter.

"What is it?" Mr. Cunnings wanted to know, worried by Will's obvious haste.

"I'll tell you when I get back down," Will replied, going straight to the stairs that led to his small bedroom.

Inside, Will changed from the more refined clothes Mr. Cunnings insisted he wear into a plain white shirt and dark breeches. Over his shirt, he buttoned a gray waistcoat. He exchanged the nice shoes he was wearing for a pair of old leather boots. Reaching under his bed, he pulled out a sword that Matthew had taught him how to construct and use. He fastened the scabbard belt over his shoulder and across his chest so the sword hung within easy reach of his right hand. Packing his Bible and extra clothes, he finally hurried back down to the shop and Mr. Cunnings.

"I must have permission to leave," Will said with great urgency. "Skye has been kidnapped by the pirates who attacked the city."

"You cannot leave when I need help here," Mr. Cunnings replied indignantly, shocking Will. "This is your job."

"If you will not allow me to go rescue someone who means a great deal to me, then you leave me no other choice. I quit," Will said with little regret and walked out the door.

He could hear Mr. Cunnings shouting behind him, warning that if he quit he would not be likely to find work anywhere else. But in light of Skye's situation, that was of little concern to Will.

Chapter Six

Will arrived at the docks just after Matthew did. "What are we going to do?" he asked, hoping his friend had a plan.

"We need to find a ship going to the island of Tortuga," Matthew said.

Will looked at him in surprise. "Why there? The island was a pirate stronghold, wasn't it?"

"Yes, and that's exactly why we're going there," Matthew answered. "We need to find a particular pirate by the name of John Morgan. Tortuga was always one of his favorite ports, and he may just be there."

Will repeated the name. "I've never heard of him."

"He's not a well-known pirate," Matthew said with a shrug. "And if he's anything like he was when we last met, he's probably gotten himself killed by now, but I'm hoping that isn't the case."

"How do you know him?"

Matthew lowered his voice with caution. "I helped him escape from being hanged."

Will's eyes widened a little. "You did? Why?"

Matthew shrugged again. "We were both young and got to be friends. I guess I didn't think he deserved hanging."

"It doesn't seem very likely that we'll find him," Will commented after a brief moment of silence.

"No it doesn't, but he's the only one I know with the means and knowledge of pirates to help us. I've got to believe that if it's God's plan for us to find him, we will and if we don't, He'll show us another way."

Will nodded, believing so as well.

Matthew glanced up and down the harbor before his gaze fell on an old trading vessel that was just being loaded up by a rough-looking crew.

"We'll try them," Matthew told Will. "They look like the most likely to take us where we need to go."

He and Will walked toward the ship, which appeared as rough and filthy as its crew. Matthew stopped just behind the man who gave the orders.

"Excuse me, sir."

The man turned to look at them with squinty eyes. He was a large man with two big tattoos on each of his broad shoulders.

"You wouldn't happen to know of any ships heading to Tortuga, would you?" Matthew asked.

The man eyed him. "Well now, that depends on why ya wanna get there and if what yer doin' is legal. Ain't no one gonna wanna get caught aidin' pirates."

"We are not pirates. We're just searching for someone," Matthew explained.

"Well, that bein' the case, we're headin' up that way. I s'pose we might consider lettin' ya off there."

"It is urgent that we find this person and if you have room on board, we'll be glad to work for our passage," Matthew offered.

The man reached up to scratch his scraggly beard. "Well, we did 'appen to lose a coupla crewmen on our last voyage, so I guess ya could 'ave the job."

"When do we sail?" Matthew asked.

"We're 'bout ready to sail now."

The thick darkness inside the ship made it difficult to tell how much time passed, but Skye could tell a new day had dawned by the sparkle of light through the crack. She hugged her knees up to her chest and laid her head on them, losing herself in her thoughts.

Some amount of time later, approaching footsteps brought her head up. When Kelley appeared with a lantern, Skye pushed to her feet. Kelley stopped at the door and stared in at her with an unnerving look of self-satisfaction that grew into a smirk.

"I received your message and instead of lettin' you slowly starve or die of thirst down here where I cannot enjoy it, I'll speed up the process and make it so the whole crew can enjoy it as well."

A chill slithered through Skye, but she made no outward reaction as Kelley unlocked the cell door. Pirates walked in and grabbed Skye by the arms. She put up a little struggle though it was hopeless. They pushed her out of the cell and led her along behind their captain. When they reached the top deck and her eyes adjusted to the light, she saw the crew busy at work.

"Listen up," Kelley called out.

Most of the men stopped what they were doing in order to listen.

"As you know, this is the girl who'll make us all rich. However, at the moment, she is unwilling to tell me where the treasure is. I'm thinkin' a day or two tied to the mast with no food or water will loosin' 'er tongue, don't you?"

With cruel enjoyment, the crew hooted and jeered as they watched the pirates take Skye to the mainmast. They put her back to it and tied ropes tightly around her. Kelley stepped in front of her and grinned maliciously.

"Now have you reconsidered?"

"No," Skye answered, her mind set.

"Very well then. Once you've changed your mind, I'll have you cut free."

Turning, he strode away to his cabin and the crew returned to their work. Skye stared at Kelley until he disappeared behind his cabin door. Then her eyes roamed the ship, wondering how long she would have to endure before Kelley freed her. He would never let her die, not if he didn't have the treasure, or at least she didn't believe he would.

Night fell on the longest three days Will had ever lived through and finally the glittering lights of Tortuga appeared in the distance. They had spent the last three days working for their passage, just as they said they would. Will had never sailed before, but learned fast. Matthew, on the other hand, proved to be an experienced sailor, though he had never mentioned sailing to Will before.

At the once-infamous pirate port, Will and Matthew prepared to leave the ship. After gathering up their belongings, they thanked the captain for allowing them to sail with him and went ashore. Glancing over his shoulder to watch the ship sail away as they walked down the dock, Will desperately hoped that even if they didn't find Matthew's friend, they could still find another way off the island. He could already tell that it was not a place where he would want to be stranded.

Once in the city, Will's feeling was compounded. Constant shouting and laughter that wouldn't cease until very late into the night filled his ears. What was worse was that there seemed to be no manner of sanitation at all. Garbage filled the streets. Though the city wasn't as heavily used by pirates as it had been in the past, many still came there. One man after another staggered past them on his way to and from the numerous taverns. Will couldn't imagine finding anyone here who could help them, but he trusted that Matthew knew what he was doing.

They had gone some distance when Matthew stopped abruptly and said in great surprise, "There he is."

Will followed Matthew's gaze to four men. Two held one man tightly between them while the fourth man stood in front of him.

"Which one?" Will wondered.

"The one who is in trouble," Matthew said wryly, shaking his head.

They took a few cautious steps closer, enough to hear the argument taking place.

"I want me money now!" shouted the man in front.

"I don't exactly have it at the moment, but I promise I'll pay you if you give me some time," John replied. "And tell ya what, I'll even give you more," he said dramatically.

"The way I see it, I should get more anyway for havin' to wait so long," the first man declared.

"What I meant was you'll get more than the more you were gonna get 'cause you'll have to wait a little longer."

In no mood to listen, the man ignored John's proposition. "I've wasted enough time."

"How 'bout I give you the map to this island where there is more treasure than you've ever seen in your life," John said, reacting hastily, dangling the prospect of treasure as his last resort. "I'll give it to you if you let me go."

"'How 'bout ya just give it to me," the man said pulling a pistol from his coat and pointing it at him.

John scrunched up his face and leaned his head back. "I don't believe I can negotiate very well with a pistol pointed in my face."

"Who said we was negotiatin'?" the man sneered. "All you have to do is give us the money and the map."

"Well, I don't exactly have either of 'em with me," John admitted.

"That's too bad, 'cause I'm through with waitin'," the man decided. He pulled back the hammer to his pistol and aimed.

Matthew took quick action. "Excuse me, gentlemen," he said walking up to them. "I have some business with this man and it won't do me any good if he's dead."

"Then ya shoulda come to 'im sooner," replied the man with the pistol.

As he moved to pull the trigger, Matthew yanked out his sword and hit the pistol, which sent it flying a few feet away. It went off and the bullet nearly hit one of the other two men. They were about to draw their swords when they noticed Will just behind Matthew, his sword drawn as well.

"Now, can we do our business with this man or will there have to be a fight?" Matthew asked.

The two men looked to their leader, who paused for a long moment.

"All right, you can do yer business," he answered finally. "But we want our money."

"Well, I'll talk to him about that, but right now it's urgent that we have his help," Matthew said.

Biding their time, the men walked off, likely heading for one of the taverns. Will and Matthew made certain they were gone before turning to John, who was obviously at least a little intoxicated.

Squinting, he asked, "Do I know you?"

Matthew sent Will an exasperated look before taking hold of John's arm and pulling him into a lighter area, giving Will a chance to see the man better. His appearance certainly left no doubt that he was a pirate. He had long, dark, poorly-kept hair and his clothes were a bit ragged around the edges, having not seen a good washing in months. Will wondered if he would truly be able to help them find Skye.

John studied Matthew in better lighting. "Oh, you," he muttered after a moment, scrunching up his face in displeasure.

"I would have expected a kindlier greeting for the man who saved your life," Matthew chided.

"Saved it!" John exclaimed loudly. "You nearly got me killed!"

Matthew's brow lowered. "You must be thinking of someone else because the way I remember it, you could have got *me* killed."

John paused for a long moment and then shrugged before studying Matthew again with narrowed, dark eyes. "You look older."

Matthew shook his head with a sigh. "If your memory serves you, you'll remember the incident was almost fifteen years ago."

John frowned, seemed to be counting, and then said, "It was, wasn't it?"

Matthew could only sigh again. "Enough remembering past events, we need to speak with you. It's urgent."

Matthew had barely spoken before lightning lit up the sky producing an earsplitting crack of thunder.

"We're not gonna stand out here, are we?" John asked, making a face and looking up at the black sky.

"Do you have a place to go?"

"Follow me," John instructed and led them even further into the city.

Skye's muscles ached and cramped. She tried to shift positions, but the ropes were too tight. She could barely feel her legs anymore, her throat cracked with thirst, and her stomach squeezed with hunger. She had been at the mast since morning the day before and her body was weakening. With growing desperation, she prayed that Kelley would soon free her.

Just as Skye began to drift off into a light sleep, a loud rumbling of thunder jolted her awake. She tipped her head to look up into a night sky which was darker than normal. Not a star could be seen. A flash of lightning lit the ship, followed by another thunder clap. Within minutes, the wind picked up fiercely, and drops of rain pelted at Skye's face. As the wind grew stronger, crewmen hurried around deck, sails billowing and straining against the rigging.

The door of Kelley's cabin burst open and Kelley strode out, scanning his ship. One of the crewmen rushed up to him and they spoke. The man then nodded and ran to where a bell hung and rang it loudly.

"All hands on deck!" he shouted over the ever-increasing roar of the wind.

Will took a seat with Matthew and John at a private table in the corner of the noisy, crowded tavern John had brought them to. The moment they entered, John had started toward the bar to get himself a mug of rum, but Matthew had stopped him, saying he'd had enough already.

"So what could possibly bring you all the way to Tortuga seekin' me after fifteen years?" John asked, still moping over the missed drink.

"Three days ago, Kingston was attacked by pirates. They kidnapped a girl from the orphanage there—"

"So?" John interrupted.

"Let me finish," Matthew stressed hastily. "She is like a daughter to me and no one is making an effort to find her."

"And you want me to help you rescue her," John said, rolling his eyes with a sigh.

"Yes."

"Sorry, but you'll have to find someone else to help you." John stood to leave.

"Hold on a minute." Matthew reached out to grab his arm, forcing him to sit back down. "I would not ask this if it wasn't extremely important to me, but please help us and repay me for saving your life."

John sighed heavily and put his head in his hands. *Now why'd he have to go an' say that?* Truth be told, he could never say no to the man who had been his only friend those fifteen years ago when he'd faced imminent hanging. He couldn't help but feel like he owed a debt, and he did vaguely remember telling Matthew that if ever he needed help, all he had to do was find him and ask.

"Oh, all right," he said in exasperation, but then added, "if you buy me a drink." He may not exactly want to help them find this girl, but at least he could get a little something out of it.

Matthew frowned, wanting strongly to deny the request, but then handed John a coin.

"Thank you," John said with a cocky grin. "I'll be right back to discuss the details."

He returned momentarily with a large mug of rum. "Okay, so tell me exactly what happened."

"As I said," Matthew began, "three days ago, pirates attacked Kingston. They blew up the fort and some of the homes nearby. A band of them evidently came ashore because they broke into the orphanage and kidnapped the girl."

"Did they raid the city or kidnap anyone else?" John wanted to know, a keen look in his eye belying his inebriated state.

"No."

"Who is this girl an' why would they want her?"

"You've heard of Daniel McHenry?"

"Of course. Anyone who knows anythin' about pirates has heard of 'im."

"The girl is Skylar McHenry, his daughter."

"I see," John said with a nod. "And let me guess. These pirates are after the famous treasure her father was said to 'ave hidden somewhere."

Matthew nodded.

"Why don'tcha just wait? When she tells 'em, they're bound to let 'er go," John said, knowing it wasn't the truth, but hoping he could get out of his agreement to help. "They'll have no use for 'er."

"You and I both know that's far from true," Matthew countered. "Even if it were, I know that these particular pirates wouldn't release her. For one thing, she promised her father she'd never tell anyone where the treasure is and nothing could make her break that promise. Number two, Daniel McHenry used to sail on this ship and he left the crew, taking a prisoner with him. The captain likely still holds a grudge, and he'll take his revenge out on Skye."

"Just who exactly are we goin' after?" John wanted to know as he took a swig of his rum and tried to recall who Daniel McHenry had sailed with.

"Captain Francis Kelley."

John nearly choked on his rum and slammed his mug back down. He looked wide-eyed at Matthew and then back at his mug.

"Okay, I think maybe you were right. I think I *have* had enough. I'm beginnin' to hear things," John said and pushed the rum away. "I could've sworn I heard you say the name Francis Kelley."

"You did."

"Okay, you did say it, and I should've known you were only jokin'," John said with a nervous laugh.

"Listen," Matthew emphasized with great seriousness. "I don't have any reason or time for jokes. Skye *was* kidnapped by Kelley, and we *are* going to rescue her."

"It's a suicide mission!" John exclaimed. "Some of the best ships in the British Navy have gone after the *Finder* and none have been able to best her. You go after Kelley and even if you happened to survive an attack on your ship, you'd be captured and killed. Kelley is by no means known for kindness to his prisoners."

"Exactly why we must rescue Skye before it's too late. And if we die trying, so be it."

John was silent for several seconds. "I'm crazy," he muttered, "but I'll still help you 'cause I can see this girl means a lot to you."

"She does," Will said after sitting silent throughout the conversation.

John looked at him critically. "I don't believe we've been introduced."

"My name is William James," Will replied. "I grew up with Skye in the orphanage."

John nodded and then turned to ask Matthew, "What exactly is it you need?"

"A ship that will take us to find Kelley and then bring us back to Kingston when we've rescued Skye," Matthew answered simply.

"I'd be changin' the *when* to *if*," John remarked. "Now about the ship. I'm lucky enough to have one at the moment, not a big one mind you, but she's fast. I also have a small crew that's been sailin' with me for a coupla years now, and I'm hopin' they're loyal enough not to jump overboard as soon as they learn what we're doin'. If that happens, I guess we're goin' after Kelley alone."

With that settled, they left the tavern. Outside, rain poured down from the inky darkness above. John led Will and Matthew quickly to his ship. It was fairly small, as he had said, but it was in good shape and appeared to be very fast. The three eagerly took shelter from the rain below deck. Matthew and John sat down at a table to talk more, but Will decided to try to get some sleep. He hadn't found much on the trip to Tortuga. Finding the hammock that John directed him to, he lay down and fell asleep.

Chapter Seven

Thick sheets of rain hammered the ship, and the masts creaked loudly as the sails strained against them. A blast of wind hit her and Skye groaned, pulling with all the strength she had left against the rough ropes that bound her to the mast. She couldn't stand up any more. She had to sit down. Resting for a moment, she could barely see the crew scurrying through the rain.

She made one last desperate attempt to loosen the ropes and finally, because of the rain slicking down the mast, they slackened a little—just enough for her to slide down and sit. Finally able to rest, Skye realized how cold she was. The rain was like ice, and she had no shelter from the wind, which set her to shivering uncontrollably.

She huddled against the mast for hours before she noticed the wind begin to die down and the rain to lessen. The ship grew brighter as the sun rose, hidden behind thick clouds. Morning had arrived after a night that had seemed as though it would never end. Soon the wind died almost to nothing, but still it rained incessantly. Most of the ship's wet and tired crew sought shelter below.

With no hope of comfort, Skye pulled her knees closer to her chest and rested her head on them. Her teeth chattered. How much longer would she have to bear it? She knew she could try pleading with Kelley, but she wouldn't. It would only give him satisfaction.

Skye didn't know whether to be relieved or apprehensive when footsteps came near. Lifting her head with what little strength she had left, she saw Kelley stop in front of her with two others.

"Is there something you want to tell me?" Kelley asked with a smirk. He didn't even consider the possibility that Skye might still oppose him.

Though exhausted, Skye's eyes burned with determination. "The treasure will never be yours," she declared hoarsely.

Kelley's smile morphed into an expression of loathing. He whipped around and nodded curtly to the pirates who hastily untied the ropes around Skye. They took her by the arms and yanked her to her feet. She barely had the strength to walk with them, but somehow she made it below. Once in her cell, she collapsed. Sleep quickly took her, and she slept soundly without waking for many hours.

Will woke to find he was alone. He looked around the cabin and listened. Voices came from above deck. Slowly, he climbed out of the hammock, and after slipping on his boots, waistcoat, and sword, he headed for the stairs. He emerged topside to find the weather warm and only remnants of clouds remained.

Scanning the ship, Will spotted John near the wheel. Matthew sat on a barrel nearby, sharpening the edge of his sword. Will walked over to him and said good morning.

"Did you sleep well?" Matthew wanted to know.

"Better than I have the last few days."

Matthew nodded in approval. "Good."

The two of them fell silent, each occupied with his own thoughts. Will watched Matthew for a moment before glancing toward the stern. His eyes caught on John who was staring at him.

"I heard you sew clothes," John said suddenly.

Will frowned. John seemed to be making fun of him.

"I worked for a tailor, if that's what you mean," Will corrected.

"And you work with soft cloth and little needles, is that right?" John asked, an unmistakable smirk creeping across his darkly-tanned face.

"What is that supposed to mean?" Will asked indignantly, not liking where this conversation was heading.

John didn't say anything at first, just kept eyeing Will with his smirk nearly turning into laughter. Finally he asked, "How can someone who does such a soft job survive out here?"

"I did not choose that job over others," Will answered, giving way to irritation. The last thing he needed on top of everything else was to be made fun of. "Mr. Cunnings was the only one I could find who would hire me."

"Uh-huh, likely story," John replied skeptically. "I'll wager you come from a wealthy family who's disowned you and you thought tailorin' would be a good job since you've never had to do a hard day's work in your life."

With this comment, Matthew quickly sought to defuse the argument.

"John, what makes you think Will isn't telling the truth?" he asked in confusion.

John shrugged. The truth was, he just liked to be difficult sometimes. It amused him. After all, meeting a young man who worked as a tailor was just too good a chance to pass up, and he didn't mean any real harm by it. He was curious to see how Will would react to his words and how far he could be pushed. John was actually a little surprised. He'd half expected Will to jump all over him at being accused of doing a woman's job. Will restrained himself quite well, better than John had expected.

"I *am* telling the truth," Will insisted. "I lived in that orphanage for fifteen years, and I never even knew my parents. Besides, tailoring isn't as easy as you think it is."

"Well, I don't see why you didn't try to find a decent, self-respectin' job," John remarked, not quite ready for the argument to come to an end.

"He did try," Matthew told him. "He worked for me as a blacksmith for a couple of years, but we didn't make enough money for both of us to live on, so I told him I wanted him to find a job he could get better pay for."

"It was not like I could go on searching until I found a job I liked," Will added, still disgruntled.

"Then tell me this," John pressed. "Why didn't you just leave the city and find a job elsewhere?"

"Besides Matthew, I'm the only friend Skye has had for the past eleven years. I would never have considered leaving."

Fearing he had nothing more to goad him with, John struggled to find another avenue of interrogation. His eyes snagged on the sword hanging at Will's side, and he nearly grinned.

"Can you even use that sword?" he asked, nodding to the weapon. "Or is it just for show?"

Will pulled it out and pointed it at John. "Can you use yours?"

Now John did grin. It was just the reaction he'd hoped for. He pulled out his own sword.

"You'll never win against me," John declared with a cocky smirk.

Will said nothing, deciding to let his skills speak for themselves.

John was first to attack, and Will parried perfectly. They traded several blows back and forth, Will's every move executed to perfection. However, he could tell that John wasn't trying very hard, so he decided to show John he could do more than just the simple moves they were trading back and forth.

Will swiftly slid his blade down John's until the point of it slid into the guard of John's sword, right above his hand. He yanked his own sword away at an odd angle, using the strength he had gained while working as a blacksmith, and sent John's sword skittering loudly down the deck. John watched in shock as it skid to a halt several feet away. Will's move had been so quick that John had not anticipated it. Finally, he took his eyes from his sword and looked into Will's smiling face.

"Luck," John muttered. "Do it again and maybe I'll take you seriously."

John retrieved his sword, and he and Will fought again. This time, John paid more attention, but as hard as he tried to keep it from happening, Will sent his sword sliding down the deck in under a minute.

"I admit," John said reluctantly, "you're pretty good, but let's see how well you do without your little tricks. Just an old-fashioned fair fight."

Will nodded.

The two faced off once more, both doing well. They tested each other skills, searching for a weakness. The duel quickly gained speed and complexity. At first John was quite confident that he had the upper hand, but soon he began to doubt himself. In just a few minutes and before John quite knew what had happened, Will had forced his sword off to the right and had his own sword pressed against John's chest. In a true fight, he would have been at Will's mercy.

Will was silent as he smiled and waited for John to speak first.

"Where'd you learn to fight like that?" John asked finally.

"Matthew and Skye," Will told him fondly.

John gawked at him. "The girl taught you?"

Will chuckled. "Yes, her father taught her a great number of useful skills when she was little. She is quite the swordswoman."

"I must say, she taught you well. Your skills are pretty impressive," John admitted with great reluctance.

Will smiled again. "Thank you."

Matthew, who now stood beside him, stared at John expectantly.

After a moment, John gave him a blank look. "What?"

"Aren't you going to apologize?" Matthew prompted. "After all, you made some pretty serious insinuations."

John rolled his eyes and sighed. "All right," he said looking at Will. "I . . . I'm sorry. But there's just one teensy little thing I would like the both of you to do for me."

He stepped forward to put his arms around Will and Matthew, pulling them close together. Speaking in a lowered voice as if someone else might hear him even though not another soul stood within many yards, he said, "Please, don't go sayin' anythin' about this to my crew when they get here."

"I won't," Will agreed with a smile. He looked around the ship. "Where are they, anyway?"

"I let 'em go ashore when we arrived here last night. They'll be back soon."

"You arrived here last night?" Will asked.

"Yes, only maybe an hour before you did," John answered.

Turning to Matthew, Will said, "I think it's quite evident God is helping us."

Matthew smiled. "Yes, indeed."

Slowly, sleep began to wear off, and Skye became aware of her surroundings. A chill ran along her body, but not the unbearable, freezing cold she had experienced while tied to the mast. Opening her eyes slowly, she focused on the side of the cell. Through the crack in the ship's side, she could see that the sun shone brightly.

With effort, Skye sat up. Her body was stiff, and her muscles ached from the strain they had suffered. Her throat was very dry and raw, and her stomach ached with a fierce hunger. As if in answer to prayer, Skye noticed a plate of food and a cup sitting by the door of her cell. *Thank You, God,* Skye offered up a quick prayer as she took the cup and drank some of the water, relieving her parched throat. Starving, she ate everything on the plate, too hungry to care what it tasted like.

Feeling considerably better, Skye tried standing. She had a bit of difficulty at first, but her legs quickly found their strength again. Walking over to the crack, she peered out. The contrasting shades of blue sky and ocean were all she could see.

With a heavy sigh, Skye sat down against the wall. She found herself realizing that she hadn't been able to read her Bible in four days, and how she missed it! Never before had she gone so long without reading.

As the hours lapsed slowly, Skye either slept or sat in thought. Many of her thoughts were of Will. She missed him more than words could describe. Skye also thought about the fact that both her parents had spent time on this very ship. She realized that she could be sitting in the very cell Kelley had kept her mother in.

Mid morning, John's crew returned to the ship. They appeared to be fairly decent men if one could call a pirate decent, though most had clearly been up half the night drinking. The test now was whether or not they'd stay when John informed them of the new plan. As he stood at the edge of the quarterdeck just above them, with Matthew and Will flanking him, John called them all together.

"Men, there's been a slight change in plans," John began good-naturedly. "I met one of me ol' friends last night, an' he needs a bit of help."

Will glanced at Matthew, wondering how the men would take it when John got into the details because so far he was making it sound like something that would be child's play.

"What do we need to do, Captain?" the first mate asked, unconcerned.

"Well, you see, this girl he's rather fond of was kidnapped, and I told 'im I'd help 'im save 'er," John answered.

"Who kidnapped 'er?"

John tried to keep a smile on his face, but it was mixed with an expression that suggested he'd been hoping no one would ask that question. Finally, he had to answer.

"Just a pirate by the name of Francis Kelley." John made the name sound like it was of little importance, but to the crew he might as well have said the devil himself.

Each of the crewmen took a step back as the group murmured all kinds of terrible rumors about Kelley. The first mate shook his head.

"We ain't about to go after the likes of Kelley. It's suicide!"

"What did I tell you?" John murmured aside to Matthew and Will, but to his men he smiled and tried to calm them. "Come now, gentlemen, just 'cause you've heard a few stories about 'im don't mean there's truth in *all* of 'em."

His words were of no comfort to the men.

"Come on, men, my friend here saved my life once. We've gotta help 'im," John pleaded.

But the first mate shook his head again. "He saved yer life, Captain, not ours. You help 'im, but leave us out of it."

John's smile and optimistic attitude disappeared, and he glowered down at the men. "Are you sayin' you've all turned your backs on me?" he said desperately, his voice a little too high.

"That ain't it at all, Captain," the first mate replied. "We haven't turned our backs on ya, we just ain't gonna risk a run in with Kelley."

"Fine," John muttered crossly. "I want all of you cowards to get your belongings and get off my ship. I'm sailin' in five minutes. Any man still aboard, stays whether he wants to or not."

The men wasted no time as they scrambled below deck to gather up their belongings. Meanwhile, Will turned to John.

"Can we sail with only three men?"

"Looks like we're gonna have to," was John's reply.

Still sore over his crew's betrayal, he began barking out orders to Matthew and Will to help him prepare for sailing, intending to make good on his threat to sail in five minutes with or without his crew. Sure enough, five minutes later, the ship sailed away from Tortuga, leaving all the crewmen standing on the dock, watching her go and talking of her certain fate.

Once they were well on their way and Matthew and Will had accomplished their tasks, something that would have been much quicker had there been a full crew, they walked up to the wheel where John stood.

"Everything seems to be in good order," Matthew informed John.

"Good," John said with a pleased smile. "You made good time too with it only bein' the two of you."

Matthew smiled while Will stared out at sea, his thoughts on Skye now that they were finally on their way to rescue her. In a moment, he turned to John with a question.

"John, what is your ship's name?"

John cast a side glance at him. "The *Good Fortune*," he said proudly.

Matthew burst into laughter and John scowled. "What's so funny?"

Matthew shook his head. "I was just thinking that some may argue over whether or not a ship with such a name fits you."

"I've had me fair share of luck over the years," John retorted sourly.

"The last time we met didn't seem to be an indicator of that."

John scoffed at the memory but then turned to Matthew, flashing a grin. "Ah, yes, but if your memory serves you, you'll remember the incident was almost fifteen years ago. A lot can happen in that time."

Matthew only grinned in return, a twinkle in his eyes, and Will watched the two of them with some amusement. He could see that John wasn't just some pirate Matthew had happened to save once, but someone who had been and still was a good friend. It made Will wonder what their story was, and he decided to ask.

"How did you two become such good friends?"

Both Matthew and John looked at him and then at each other.

"You should tell 'im," John decided after a moment. "You probably remember it better than I do."

Agreeing that was probably true, Matthew looked back to Will. "Soon after I left England, I came here to the Caribbean and was doing some work repairing cells in the local fort where I lived. John was a prisoner there and the only company I had while I worked. One day we started talking and soon became friends." He glanced at John with a grin. "Looking back though, I think John's mind was more on how he could use me to escape than on becoming friends."

John shrugged. "I won't try to deny that that was my original intent, but I got to like talkin' to you."

Matthew only chuckled and continued. "In a few days I decided I'd always regret it if I didn't help him escape, so I brought him a knife to pick the lock of his cell. I was going to help him sneak out of the fort, but that's where he came up with his own plan." Matthew pinned his eyes on John accusingly. "I had my back turned and then suddenly there was nothing. I woke up on the floor some time later with several soldiers around me."

"I can explain," John inserted quickly. "I didn't want anyone to know you helped me, so I had to make it look like you had nothin' to do with it. I figured that was the best way. I did leave that note in your pocket to apologize."

"You hit me quite hard, though," Matthew quibbled.

John smiled sheepishly. "I wanted to make sure I wouldn't have to hit you again."

Matthew laughed. "Oh, I see."

Silence followed for a short time until John began quizzing Matthew.

"So now, how exactly are you plannin' to find the girl? As of yet, you haven't told me where we're sailin', and I need to know where we're goin'. Do you know where Kelley is headed?"

"Actually, we don't," Matthew informed him slowly. "This is about as far as my plan goes. I'm trusting God for the rest."

John made a noise of disbelief. "That's trustin' a lot, don'tcha think?"

"No, I don't. He has complete control of the situation, and if He wants us to find her, we will."

John sighed as if he'd heard it all before. "If He's in control, why would He let an innocent girl be kidnapped in the first place?"

Matthew shook his head. "I don't know, but I do know that it wasn't merely chance that Will and I happened to arrive in Tortuga at nearly the same time you did even after all the years that have gone by since we last saw each other. I believe there's a reason that you and I became friends and I was able to save you. Perhaps God helped me save your life then because He knew I'd need your help now."

"It's all a very intriguing thought, but for now, I'm just gonna rely on luck," John said, dismissing Matthew's beliefs.

Matthew glanced at Will and shrugged slightly. He had tried, same as he had fifteen years ago, but he never seemed to get anywhere with John. Still, he'd never give up on his friend. Who knew what God had planned for him?

Chapter Eight

The sun had just passed its peak as early afternoon crept in the next day. Below deck, Skye paced her dark cell. She had found one of the worst parts of being held captive was the endlessness of doing nothing. It had been nearly twenty-four hours since anyone had come down to her cell. She was plagued by hunger, thirst, and the longing to be free. How she missed Will! The thought of never seeing him again was unbearable, and discouragement tried to overwhelm her. But she forced those feelings away by reciting all the Bible verses and hymns she had memorized.

When another hour had passed, Skye started to think she'd be neglected for yet another day, but then came the sound of footsteps. She turned to see the two pirates who always did Kelley's bidding. They quickly went through the usual process of taking her out of her cell and bringing her up to the deck. Kelley was waiting for them, an evil grin that filled Skye with dread plastered on his ruthless face.

"I see you've recovered quickly," he commented.

Skye just stared at him.

"Tell me, do you think your recovery will be as swift after being tied to the mast a second time?" Kelley taunted. "That's what I'll do if you do not tell me where the treasure is, and this time you'll stay there longer."

Although Skye wasn't certain she could endure the horribleness again, she refused to consider breaking her promise.

"If you want to have me die of thirst, then so be it. I will not tell you anything," Skye declared.

Kelley's eyes darkened, burning with intense fury. Never had he anticipated having this much trouble with her.

"You're as stubborn as your father," he muttered darkly.

"My father was a great man and if you are saying that I am anything like him, then I take that as a compliment," Skye retorted.

Outraged, Kelley raised his arm and backhanded her soundly. Skye winced and touched her face lightly. Looking back to Kelley, she was still determined as ever.

"You've also inherited your father's quick tongue and that got 'im into serious trouble, as it will you," Kelley warned in tight-lipped anger. "Now tell me where the treasure is right now!" he bellowed. The dangerous edge to his voice was one few would dare to mess with.

Skye drew in a deep breath and tried to stop her mind from creating a mental image of what Kelley might do. "No."

Upon hearing that word and the determination still behind it, Kelley reached the limit of his patience. *If that girl thinks she's seen the worst of what I can do, she's gravely mistaken*, Kelley raged inwardly. He looked at the two pirates on either side of Skye.

"Bind her hands to the mast," he ordered.

He stormed off toward his cabin as the pirates shoved Skye to the mainmast with an eerie rush of anticipation. Tightly, they bound her wrists so that she was facing it. With a prickle of apprehension, she turned her head to look back at Kelley's cabin. He burst back out with something in his hand. Just as Skye had feared, it was a whip. Her heart pounded rapidly as he drew near.

When Kelley stood over her, seeming taller and more intimidating than usual, he warned in a low voice, "This is your last chance, girl. It's either the treasure or . . ." he held up the whip, "this."

Skye stared at the fearsome instrument of torture, coiled up like a snake about to strike. She swallowed hard and turned her eyes away. For once, her words caught in her throat. She could not bring herself to speak.

"Fine," Kelley muttered, stepping behind her.

Skye took a shaky breath and prepared herself as best she could for the agonizing pain she knew would follow. *Please, God, help me*, she prayed desperately, her spirit quailing.

Taking a step up to the bow of the ship, Will stared out at the sparkling blue water that stretched out in every direction as far as he could see. Skye was somewhere out there in that immense, seemingly empty space. Nearly every waking moment, Will prayed for God to guide their ship to her, knowing that without His help they could never hope to find her.

Finally, Will took his eyes from the ocean and glanced over his shoulder to where Matthew had taken over at the helm, giving John some time to inspect his ship. John erupted in laughter and Will could not help but smile as he wondered what Matthew had said that John found so funny.

But in the midst of that easy humor, Will's smile disappeared. Quite suddenly he was struck by intense worry for Skye as though something were not right. Looking back out to sea, Will knew only one thing could be done. He closed his eyes and prayed quietly. "God, I don't know why I feel like this or if Skye really is in trouble—only You know. But if she is, please protect her. Please don't let Kelley harm her . . ."

Kate shifted uneasily. She stared at Skye as Kelley raised the whip, amazed at the young woman's fierce determination to stay true to her promise. Kate knew from experience just how much resolve was needed to stand up to Kelley. At the last moment, though she knew interfering with Kelley was a very unwise move, everything inside her told Kate that she could not just stand by and let Skye go through with this.

"Captain!" she called just as Kelley was about to bring the whip down.

Kelley spun around furiously. "What do you want?" he snarled. "Do you want a taste of the whip next?"

Kate cringed inside. She had already experienced the force of his anger before and had no desire to experience it again.

"I need to speak with you." She spoke boldly, hiding any doubts that clawed at her.

Kelley only glared. "Well?" he demanded after a long moment.

"In private," Kate informed him.

Kelley's glare intensified, but finally, muttering curses under his breath, he turned and stormed toward his cabin, expecting Kate to follow. She did so slowly, wondering just what she was getting herself into and why. Stepping inside the cabin, Kate closed the door and waited, watching Kelley, whose back was turned. As soon as he heard the door shut, Kelley spun to face her.

"Whatever is so important that you would dare interrupt me?"

"I was thinkin' about the girl," Kate said, keeping her voice calm. "What if she doesn't tell you anything? She could die. Either from the beatin' itself or from infection. If she dies, the location of that treasure'll be gone forever."

"She may last the first couple lashes, but once she's had a few, she'll start talkin'," Kelley stated confidently.

"But how do you know?" Kate stressed, trying to worry him. "I've heard you mention how stubborn Daniel McHenry was and obviously the girl is the same way. She hasn't said anything up to this point. What makes you so sure she'll tell you now?"

"Well, I guess we'll just have to find out," Kelley snapped. He was about to leave the cabin, but Kate stopped him.

"I've got a better idea. Let me gain her trust and I bet she'll tell me where the treasure is."

"Just how do you plan to accomplish that?"

"Let her stay with me. She'll think I talked you into it and that'll make her trust me."

Kelley's eyes narrowed shrewdly as he considered her words. Finally, he decided, "I'll give you a week. If you don't find out by then, I'm takin' the whip to both of ya."

Kate wasn't given a chance to respond before Kelley continued.

"But I'm not about to let her get off with nothin'. If she ain't gonna be in that cell then she's gonna work. She's gonna work until I get that treasure or until she drops. Now go out there, get her changed into somethin' she can work in, and get her to work, do you understand?"

Kelley stormed out of the cabin before Kate could answer. She watched him go and contemplated the deal. A week was not much time. Feeling a grave burden, she left the cabin as well and walked toward Skye.

"The captain has decided not to continue," Kate informed the pirates who still stood waiting. They groaned in disappointment before going back to their work, leaving Kate and Skye alone.

Skye raised her eyes to Kate. This pirate had saved her, at least for the moment, from the beating she wasn't quite sure she wasn't still going to get. However, she was an answer to prayer, and Skye silently thanked God.

Kate pulled a dagger from her belt and sliced through the ropes that bound Skye.

"Come with me," Kate instructed once she was free.

Confused, Skye followed her below deck and into a little, private cabin, which was bare except for a small bed at one end and an old trunk at the other.

When Kate had closed the door, Skye finally asked the only question on her mind. "Why did you stop Kelley?"

Kate said nothing at first, but then she softened. "I feel sorry for anyone who gets a beating like that, unless I think they deserve it."

"And you don't think I do?"

Kate looked Skye full in the eyes. "No, I don't."

"Thank you, Kate," Skye said, very grateful.

Kate didn't answer, but nodded. For a moment, she looked Skye up and down. "You need to change outta that dress."

Skye glanced down at her clothes, wondering what was going on. "What do you mean?"

"The captain has decided that instead of puttin' you back down in that cell, you'd be more beneficial doin' some work and you can't very well do that in a dress."

Kate went to the trunk and pulled out clothes. "Here, these oughta fit," she said. "Put 'em on."

Removing her old dress, Skye could hardly believe that Kelley was not going to lock her back up, but she wasn't about to question it. Taking the clothes from Kate, she put on the dark breeches that ended just below her knees, then the clean white shirt and dark brown waistcoat over it. She buckled a thick leather belt around her waist and finally slipped on a pair of leather boots that came up to where the breeches ended. It was the first time in eleven years she'd worn anything but a dress.

"Amazing what a change of clothes can do to your appearance," Kate remarked. "I never could picture you as a pirate 'til now."

"Well," Skye began thoughtfully, "I never considered myself a pirate. My father and the rest of the crew only stole from other pirates, and we returned what we could to the people it had been stolen from."

Kate simply nodded and a brief silence followed before she said, "We'd better get back on deck. Captain expects you to be workin,' so if you don't start soon he may change his mind."

Skye followed Kate back out of the cabin. It turned out that Kelley was waiting for them on deck. He glared furiously at Skye.

"Listen up," he barked. "I want you to scrub every inch of this deck. You won't be gettin' any sleep 'til ya do." He narrowed his eyes at Kate. "And since you dared to interrupt me before, you can help 'er. I don't care if you're up all night; this deck had better be sparklin' by mornin'. Do you understand?"

"Aye, Captain," Kate answered quietly.

Skye remained silent. Kelley threw one last glare in her direction before storming off. With no desire to press their luck, Skye and Kate quickly went to work. As they began scrubbing, Skye glanced at Kate.

"I'm sorry that you had to do this too," she apologized.

Kate shook her head. "Don't be. I would've been the one to do it whether I interrupted the captain or not."

"Why you?" Skye asked.

Kate sighed. "Well, I'm not a willing member of his crew. I guess ya might say that I'm a slave."

Skye nodded, figuring as much. "How did you come to be here?"

Kate glanced around and then answered in a hushed voice, "I think that's a story to save for when we're alone. Captain doesn't like to hear me talk about it."

Skye nodded again and focused on her work.

A short time after Will prayed for Skye, he left the bow and walked back to where Matthew now stood alone at the helm, John having disappeared somewhere below deck. Matthew greeted him and was silent for a few moments, his eyes trained on the sea. But when his gaze turned back, Will knew clearly that something was on his mind.

"Will, there's something I have meant to tell you since we left Kingston. I guess now is as good a time as any, but I'm sure it's going to be quite a shock to you."

Will frowned, concern in his expression. "What is it?"

"You don't know my last name, do you?"

Will thought about it for a moment and realized he didn't. He and Skye had only ever known Matthew by his first name. "No, I don't. Why do you ask me this now?"

"Because that means you don't really know who I am."

"What do you mean?" Confused, Will wondered if his world was about to be rocked yet again. "Who are you?"

Matthew sighed. "Will . . . my last name is McHenry."

Will's eyes went wide. "Are you related to Skye?"

Matthew nodded. "Daniel McHenry was my older brother. I am Skye's uncle."

Will stared at Matthew in stunned disbelief, not sure what to say. When he didn't speak, Matthew continued. "The reason I didn't tell you and Skye before this is because I had heard about the treasure and was afraid something like this would happen. I thought that if I kept my identity a secret, I could better keep Skye safe and no one would suspect me. If I could have, I would have adopted Skye. I've tried the best I know how to keep her safe, but as the years have passed, I let my guard down unintentionally and now the very thing I feared has happened."

Will knew now that Matthew struggled with the feeling that he was partly responsible for Skye's abduction.

"Matthew, it is not your fault that Skye was kidnapped. There was nothing you or I could have done to save her. Kelley attacked and left so quickly there was no way anyone could have known what was happening and been able to stop him . . . no matter how badly we wish we could have."

Bent over the heavy holystones, scraping them back and forth to rid the deck of dried-on salt was exhausting, but Skye actually found it preferable to being locked in her cell. It also helped that she was so used to scrubbing the floors in the orphanage, though scrubbing salt off the deck was a lot more difficult. However, what she had done in the orphanage made her a faster worker than many would have thought. Kelley had expected Skye and Kate to be at work late into the night, but they finished shortly after eight o'clock and were sent below deck to rest. Kate offered to share her cabin with Skye, which she gladly accepted.

As Skye lay down on the bed she'd made on the floor, she looked up to where Kate lay in her bunk.

"Can you tell me now how you came to be here?"

Kate sighed, staring up at the ceiling. "I am actually the captain of a ship called the *Half Moon*."

Skye propped herself up on her elbow so she could see Kate better. "Really?"

Kate nodded. "One night me an' my crew went ashore to replenish supplies. Kelley was also there. He had lost some of his crew in a storm, so he was tryin' to find men to replace 'em. They must have seen me at one of the taverns and decided that they wanted me as part of the crew. They caught me alone, captured me, and brought me here.

"My crew tried to come after me. I saw the *Half Moon* behind us once a couple of days after I was captured, but she lost us in a storm, and I haven't seen 'er since. That was eleven months ago. I keep tryin' to find a way off this ship, but Kelley keeps a close watch on me." She shook her head. "I haven't set foot on land since I've been here. Kelley never lets me go ashore when we make port."

"I'm sorry, Kate," Skye said after a moment, feeling sympathy for her. "I hope you find a way to escape."

Kate sighed again and thought about the deal she had made with Kelley. "So do I."

Chapter Nine

The days slipped passed as Skye was permitted to work as part of the crew. Kelley worked her hard; however, Skye didn't complain. Though most of the work was exhausting, in a way she enjoyed it. The fear of Kelley overshadowed everything, but Skye loved sailing and could not help but feel at home again on the sea. Everything she had learned as a child came back to her quickly. Within a day, she was working with the swiftness and incredible ease that could only be achieved by her years of practice and her own natural gift for sailing. As cruel and heartless as the rest of the crew was, they had grudgingly become quite impressed with her.

Kate came to be a very close friend to Skye and that friendship was invaluable. Not only did she not feel as alone on the ship, but Skye also realized that Kate was the first woman she'd had to talk to as a friend since her mother died.

Six days after Kate saved Skye from Kelley's beating, the two of them returned to their cabin for the night after the long day's work. While she prepared for bed, Skye glanced questioningly at Kate. She had been unusually quiet throughout the day, and Skye had yet to find a reason.

"Is there something wrong, Kate?" she asked finally.

Kate stopped what she was doing and sighed heavily. She turned to Skye, her expression hesitant. "Yes, there is," she answered in a quiet voice.

Skye frowned. "What is it?"

"I meant to tell you this, and I should've before now. The day Kelley was gonna whip you, he only stopped 'cause I made a deal with him."

"What kind of deal?"

"I told him that I'd gain your trust and have you tell me where your treasure is."

Skye stared at her, wondering for a moment if Kate's friendliness had all been an act.

"But that was never my true intent," Kate quickly explained. "I only made the deal to buy us some time, but now our time is up."

"What do you mean?"

Kate looked at Skye gravely. "Kelley gave me one week to find out where your treasure is or . . . he'd whip both of us. The week ends tomorrow. I've been tryin' all week to find a way for us to escape, but how can you get off a ship in the middle of the ocean?"

Skye exhaled heavily and bowed her head in despair. She then looked back up at Kate. "I'm so sorry you ended up to be part of this. You should never have stopped him."

Kate shook her head. "No, I'm glad I did. I'm not afraid of him and can take whatever he gives me. He's beaten me before, and I know he won't be that severe because he wants me to keep workin'. You're the one I fear for. Kelley won't hold back with you. As long as he gets what he wants, it doesn't matter if you die in the end. That would only please him more."

"I will not tell him," Skye said determinedly.

"Are you sure, Skye?" Kate asked. "Are you sure that in the end you'll be able to hold out?"

For the first time, Skye truly considered just how much pain she could endure.

"Skye, as a friend, I think you should just tell Kelley where the treasure is. Is it really worth goin' through all this?"

"It is not the treasure that's important to me, Kate. It's the promise I made to my father. It's the last promise I ever made to him, and I just can't break it," Skye said earnestly, helping Kate to understand. "And now, even more than that, I realize that promise is what's kept me alive. If I tell Kelley where the treasure is, he will have no need for me anymore, and he'll surely kill me. For that reason I *must* not tell him."

Kate realized Skye was right and didn't know what to say. It all seemed hopeless.

Neither Skye nor Kate could sleep that night. Kate stared at the ceiling silently from where she lay in her bunk, as her mind worked desperately to form a plan to stall Kelley. A couple of feet away, Skye sat on her little bed on the floor, head bowed and hands clasped before her, asking God to save both Kate and herself.

"I wish I had my Bible," Skye murmured sadly after a while. "Reading it always comforts me during my most difficult times."

Kate glanced at her but said nothing.

Skye's hand went to a little metal object that hung on a black cord around her neck. It was something she had managed to keep hidden all the time she was on the *Finder*. Carefully, she unhooked the tiny clasps at the end of the cord and held the object out to look at it. A small, metal cross glittered in the moonlight that filtered into the room through the tiny, round window. With a faint, wistful smile, she fondly ran her fingers along its smooth surface. She took her eyes from it when Kate's voice broke through her faraway thoughts.

"What is that?"

Skye held up the necklace so Kate could see that it was a cross. "My best friend gave it to me a couple of years ago. He has one just like it."

Will lay awake in his hammock, unable to find sleep. All of his thoughts were on Skye as he stared at the small cross of the necklace he held. So lost in his thoughts of her, he was startled to hear Matthew come below deck to get some rest before relieving John at the helm.

"Where did you get that?" Matthew asked curiously.

Will glanced at him briefly before his eyes went to the cross again. "I made it once when I still worked for you. I made one for Skye too. She always wears it, so she must have it with her."

Matthew smiled a little. "I'm sure it's a comfort to her."

Will nodded and, after a moment, let out a heavy sigh. "I wish it could have been me in Skye's place. I can't stand the thought of what might have happened to her, having been in Kelley's hands all this time."

Matthew put his hand on Will's shoulder. "I wish the same thing, but God's plans are different. Remember, Skye isn't only in Kelley's hands, but God's too."

At the dreaded light of dawn, Skye and Kate slowly rose from their beds. Skye pulled on her boots and waistcoat before leaning back against the wall, grasping her necklace. She took a deep breath, asking God to help her face Kelley when the time came.

"Are you ready?" Kate asked.

Skye looked at her and nodded. Opening the door, they reluctantly left the cabin and went about their work on deck. Skye kept a wary eye on the door of Kelley's cabin, dreading what would come when he woke. All she could do was keep praying and hope that God would again answer her prayers.

The newly-risen sun shimmered warmly on John's back as he stood at the ship's wheel. He glanced over his shoulder to look at it before again staring straight ahead with a sense of foreboding. Dark, angry-looking clouds filled the horizon, and he knew from many long years of experience that this wouldn't be just any typical storm at sea. This one would be dangerous. Feeling the wind grow slightly stronger, John looped a rope around the wheel to keep it from turning and hurried over to the hatchway that led below.

"Matthew, Will, you two better come on deck!" he called.

A few moments later, Matthew and Will emerged.

"What is it, John?" Matthew asked.

"We're in for some rough weather," John said grimly. "And without a crew, it's gonna take a miracle to keep the *Fortune* afloat."

Dawn aged an hour, though one could barely tell since it was still so dark. Thick, gray clouds filled the sky and everyone knew a storm would erupt very soon. Skye stared up at them and she, like John, knew the storm would be severe.

Her eyes were pulled away from the clouds at the alarming creak of Kelley's cabin door. Skye's blood turned to ice as she watched him walk out from her position near the bow. The evil pirate captain scanned the ship. Skye's heart sank when he called for Kate. Throwing a remorseful glance at Skye, Kate left her work and walked over to him. He ordered her into the cabin and walked in after her, closing the door. A long, agonizing minute passed, and Skye's heart pounded, her entire body tingling with an innate sense of fear.

Finally, the door burst open with a loud bang, and Kelley stormed out. The whip dangled from his hand. Kate hurried out behind him, pleading for more time, but her words were ignored. Kelley searched the deck, eyes burning with a rage that Skye could see even from where she stood.

"Bring me the girl!" he bellowed.

Not wanting to be dragged over to Kelley by the other pirates, Skye walked toward him, offering up a prayer, begging God to give her the strength she needed.

"I'm right here, Kelley," she said, halting in front of him and working to suppress her fears.

Looming over her, Kelley demanded, "Where is it?"

Skye glanced at Kate, whose expression was of complete helplessness, before looking up at Kelley and answering with all the confidence she could, "We've been through this before, and my answer is no different from what it was then. I will not break my promise to my father."

Kelley's face turned red with anger. He grabbed Skye's arm and dragged her to the mainmast. When they reached it, he took hold of the back of Skye's waistcoat and ripped it off of her, leaving her wearing only the thin white shirt. In a moment, her hands were tied once again around the mast.

Kelley glared down at her. "I don't think you even deserve to be given one last chance to tell me what I want to know before I beat it out of you," he growled.

Skye stared up at him. Though she knew Kelley was likely to be even more cruel than he would have been last time, she found that her fear wasn't as great.

"Even if you offered it, Kelley, I wouldn't take it."

Outrage burned in Kelley's eyes at the fact that Skye was still so defiant despite what was about to happen to her. In the midst of his anger, his evil mind formed an idea, and he grabbed Skye's long, braided hair, yanking her head back.

"I imagine you've been growin' this out all your life, haven't you?"

This time, Skye didn't speak, sick at the thought of what he was going to do. With her silence, Kelley taunted, "Wouldn't it be a terrible shame if suddenly it was gone?"

He pulled out a dagger. Its sharp edge scraped against the back of Skye's neck as Kelley placed it under her hair.

"This is for how long you've defied me."

Kelley put pressure on the dagger, and the sickening sound of her hair being cut filled Skye's ears. Short pieces fell into her face as he cut the last of it. Tears stung her eyes at the thought of what he had done, but Skye told herself to put that sorrow aside for now because her hair was the least of her worries.

As Skye's dark braid fell to the deck at Kelley's feet, he noticed something else. Skye felt him take hold of the cord around her neck, and she realized with horror that he had found her necklace. He yanked it off her and looked at it. When he saw that it was a cross, he laughed cruelly.

"You think your God can save you from this?"

Skye straightened and looked at him, her face set with fierce determination. "He did last time, and if it is His will to do so this time, then no one can stop Him."

Kelley laughed even louder and tossed Skye's necklace away. She knew with sorrow that she'd probably never see the treasured gift again.

"I would like to see Him try to stop me," Kelley declared arrogantly, moving to take a position behind Skye.

He raised the whip, and Skye braced herself. *Oh, God, please give me the strength I need . . .* A split second later, Skye's breath was taken by an intense burning unlike any pain she had ever experienced as the whip easily cut through her shirt and into her left shoulder and her back. She fought to stay on her feet and hold back the cry of pain that so desperately wanted to escape from inside of her. She succeeded, but Skye knew that very soon it would not be possible.

Kelley raised the whip again, and Skye struggled to prepare herself while still trying to bear the pain from the first lash. However, before Kelley could bring it down, a bolt of lightning sizzled through the clouds followed by a deafening crack of thunder that seemed nearly loud enough to split the ship. Without warning, the wind picked up, billowing the sails, and great drops of rain pelted the deck. Kelley had no choice but to drop the whip and give his men orders as the storm rapidly intensified. Thick sheets of rain soaked through everything and savage gusts of wind nearly took people off their feet. Lightning flashed and thunder vibrated through the wooden vessel.

The muffled shouting of the men could hardly be heard over the wind, and Skye could barely make out their dark forms. Then a loud crack of wood splintering came from overhead and the mast shuddered. If it fell, she would likely be killed by it. She yanked desperately on the ropes around her wrists, but they would not budge. Just as panic took hold, someone grabbed her arm. Relief washed over her when she recognized Kate who pulled out a knife and cut the ropes.

Pulling her up, Kate shouted over the wind, "We have to help keep her afloat or we'll all end up at the bottom of the ocean!"

Skye followed Kate over to where some rigging was loose and being whipped around by the wind. She reached out to grab one of the ropes and quickly tied it down. Just as she and Kate had tied down the last line, a huge wave crashed over the ship. Skye tried to grab the railing, but it was too late. The wave swept her across the deck, and she slammed into the railing on the other side. As soon as the water receded, she stood up.

"Kate!" she called.

Searching frantically, Skye heard her name from farther down the deck. Turning, she spotted Kate hanging from the side of the ship. Skye ran over to her and took Kate's arm, pulling with all the strength she had. Kate was nearly to safety when another wave came roaring toward them. She tightened her grip on Kate's arm and the railing, but both were yanked away from her when the wave crashed down on top of them. Before she knew it, Skye was plunged into the raging sea. She swam for the surface, but she reached it only long enough to take a breath of air before the churning waves forced her back under.

For several minutes, she fought just to stay above water long enough to get the air she needed. When she was able to stay up a little longer, she searched the stormy sea. The *Finder* was nowhere in sight and neither was Kate. Skye called her name, but she could barely hear her own voice over the sound of the ocean.

Still she kept trying, but it was growing ever harder to stay above water as her strength diminished. An eternity seemed to pass, and Skye knew she could not fight against the sea for much longer. Just as she felt she had nothing left to give, her feet found solid ground, and she pulled herself up onto land. Crawling behind a rock that towered above her and shielded her from the wind, she collapsed in exhaustion as the rain continued to beat down from the sky.

Chapter Ten

At last, Skye woke again, greeted not by the roaring wind or freezing rain, but by the sound of gentle waves and the warmth of the sun shining down upon her. She scanned what little was in her view and started to push herself up but stopped abruptly, clenching her teeth with a groan. Her shoulder burned with an intense pain made many times worse by the salt from the ocean water that had entered the wound. Careful not to use her left arm, she pushed to her feet.

Taking stock of her situation, Skye cast her eyes critically over the area. Directly in front of her stretched out a white sand beach littered with seaweed and other debris from the storm. Several yards ahead stood a thick, palm tree jungle. What lay beyond she could not know. Leaving that mystery for the moment, Skye turned to look out to sea. Raising her good arm to shield her eyes from the glare of the sun, she could see nothing but the white caps of the waves.

She felt very alone and remembering Kate, Skye looked up and down the beach for any sign of her friend.

"Kate!" she called.

Her only answer came from the mournful cries of the gulls circling above her. Knowing Kate could be elsewhere on the Island, Skye walked along the beach to see what she could find and prayed that Kate had reached safety. Twenty minutes of searching and calling produced nothing, and Skye feared that Kate had not made it to the island, which meant she had either drowned or somehow made it back to the *Finder*.

Yet, just when Skye had given up hope, her name came from the trees and Kate emerged from the forest. Skye spoke her name in relief and hurried to meet her.

"I've been searchin' all over for you," Kate told her. "I was hopin' maybe you'd taken shelter in the trees."

Skye shook her head. "I was in some rocks farther down the beach."

"Are you all right?" Kate asked, looking her over.

"Except for my shoulder, yes, I think I'm fine."

"Here, come with me," Kate directed. "Lucky for us, I found some fresh water. We should do what we can to clean your wound before it becomes infected."

Skye followed Kate into the jungle. Pausing briefly along the way, Kate bent down and picked a few leaves from a small plant.

"What are those for?" Skye asked curiously.

"They're used for healing," Kate answered. "They'll fight against infection."

"Where did you learn that?"

"One of the crewmen on my ship used to be a native doctor. He taught us what plants can be used for healing and other medical purposes."

Shortly, they came upon a small, crystal clear spring surrounded by tropical ferns and brightly-colored flowers.

"Why don't you sit down?" Kate said.

95

Skye sat at the edge of the spring. The still water was like a perfect mirror, and she stared at her reflection. It was her first look at her hair since Kelley had cut off her braid. Her hair now reached only slightly past her chin.

Kate noticed Skye looking at herself. "It's not that bad," she encouraged.

"No, it isn't," Skye agreed. "I'm thankful to have escaped before Kelley did any worse."

With a nod, Kate lifted the back of Skye's blood-stained shirt, revealing the long, bloody cut that ran from her shoulder to the middle of her back. Her shoulder was also dark with bruises from smashing into the *Finder's* railing during the storm.

Tearing a piece of cloth from her waistcoat, Kate dipped it into the spring.

"I'm afraid this'll hurt," she warned.

"I know," Skye said, bracing herself.

Kate cleaned the wound gently, careful not to cause Skye more pain than was necessary. Skye winced and drew in her breath. When finally Kate had finished, Skye's wound was not nearly so painful now that the salt had been cleaned out of it. Kate pulled open the leaves she had picked and applied the liquid from inside of them to the cut. It stung, but Skye knew she could not risk getting an infection here on this island where no one could help them.

When Kate had finished, they both stood and took in their surroundings.

"We should head back to the beach," Kate said. "The only way off this island is for someone to find us, and the only way for anyone to know we're here is to start a signal fire."

"How are we going to start one?" Skye asked.

A smile came to Kate's face as she reached into a hidden pocket in one of her boots. Out of it, she pulled a dagger and a piece of flint. "I was always afraid that Kelley would finally get sick of havin' me around and maroon me on some island, so I made sure I was prepared."

Skye smiled in return, and they walked away to the beach, gathering whatever dry wood and old palm fronds they could find along the way. It was not long before they had a good-sized fire burning.

"Now all we have to do is hope a ship passes by and sees it," Kate said, throwing a few more pieces of wood into the flames.

"I have been praying that one will," Skye told her.

"Well then, let's hope God answers your prayers."

"He has so far." Skye looked at Kate, gauging her reaction. "The storm was one of His answers. He saved both you and me from Kelley just as I asked Him to."

"He may have saved us from Kelley, but He put us here," Kate stated dryly.

"He put us here alive and uninjured," Skye corrected gently. "We could just as easily have drowned. I'd far rather be here than with Kelley, and I believe that God will provide a way off this island."

"I hope you're right." Kate was silent for a moment as she stared at the fire. Finally, she turned back to Skye. "I forgot to give you this earlier."

Kate pulled an object from her pocket, and Skye's eyes lit up with a smile of joy as Kate handed it to her. It was the cross necklace Will had made for her.

"I picked it up when the storm hit," Kate told her. "I knew it meant a lot to you."

Skye gave her a grateful smile. "Thank you, Kate. It does mean a lot to me, and I didn't think I'd ever see it again." She rubbed her fingers tenderly over the cross before tying the ends safely around her neck.

When the fire was big enough to stay burning for a while, Skye and Kate trekked into the jungle to look for food. Coconuts lay everywhere, but to try to open them seemed like more trouble than it was worth since they had fresh water. They were very happy to find several fruit trees hanging with sweet, ripe fruit. Upon seeing them, Skye thanked God for providing them with all the food and water they would need to survive on the island for however long they remained.

Picking what they needed for the day, Skye and Kate returned to the beach and sat under the cool shade of the trees, watching the horizon intently for any sign of ships. For a long time, they sat in a companionable silence while their minds wondered over the events of the last couple of weeks. The unsettling memories Skye carried from being on the *Finder* would be with her for the rest of her life. No doubt it was one of her most difficult trials, aside from the deaths of her parents, but she was incredibly thankful it had not been worse. Kelley could have done so much more to her than he had, but God had been with her, and she knew His protection had kept her safe.

Finally, when their thoughts turned away from their ordeal, Skye and Kate started to talk. Skye told Kate stories about sailing with her father, and Kate told her briefly of some of the voyages she'd made on the *Half Moon*. After that, they took turns resting while the other kept a watchful eye on the fire and the ocean.

When the day turned into evening and the sun sank low, painting the sky a brilliant orange and pink, Skye and Kate watched it from their places under the trees. Admiring the beauty of it, she thought of her father and how much he would have loved to be there with her. Watching the sunsets together had been something they had always enjoyed while sailing. Now those times were precious memories.

After a moment, Skye sighed heavily and glanced at Kate. "What was the worst moment of your life?"

Kate frowned. "Where did that question come from?"

Skye shrugged. "I don't know. I'm just curious."

So long a silence followed that Skye didn't expect Kate to answer and was surprised when Kate spoke.

"I was six years old," she began. "Me an' my mother were part of a group of slaves bein' sold at a slave market. I was too young to fully realize that we might be separated, so I wasn't prepared when it happened. She was sold to one person, and I was sold to another. I've been through a lotta things, but watchin' them take my mother away has to be the worst."

"That is something we have in common," Skye said with sadness in her voice. "The last time I ever saw my father was the worst moment of my life. I was aware that he could be captured and killed, but I failed to prepare myself for it because I never believed it would happen. Knowing that night that in a few hours I'd be all alone except for God was a feeling I never want to feel again."

"So you have no relatives?" Kate asked.

"My grandfather lives in Kingston, but he has never acknowledged me as his granddaughter. Because of my father," Skye explained.

"And no one would adopt you for the same reason," Kate said knowingly.

Skye nodded.

"There, another thing we have in common. Few people truly care about us 'cause of who we are. You're the daughter of a pirate, and I'm an African."

"But at least God cares about everyone, no matter who they are. As for people, well, I am blessed enough to have met two who have always cared a great deal about me."

"Who are they?"

Skye looked at Kate, hesitance coming to her face. She trusted her, but she still was reluctant to give up the names of her beloved friends. Kate realized her reluctance and said, "I promise, I would never tell anyone."

By the sincere tone of her voice and the seriousness of her eyes, Skye believed her.

"About two months after coming to the orphanage, I met a boy named Will. He has always been the closest friend I've ever had. He's the one who made and gave me my necklace."

That piqued Kate's interest. "How did you meet him?"

"Some of the other children were tormenting me about my father having been hanged when Will stood up for me. He was the first one who ever did that," Skye remembered fondly. "He's always taken care of me and been there when I've needed him." She paused, eyes focusing out at the ocean though it was not what her mind was seeing. "I miss him so much. It seems like such a long time since I last saw him though it really hasn't been."

Kate witnessed the same look in Skye's eyes that she too had once had while thinking about someone who'd meant everything to her. Not wishing to disturb Skye's thoughts, she sat silent until Skye came back to reality and remembered she had been answering Kate's question.

"My other friend is a man named Matthew. Will and I met him in church when I was twelve. He reminds me so much of my father. They look and act so much alike."

"Why didn't he adopt you?"

"He wanted to, but his business is very poor, and he couldn't make enough money to support both of us."

For a short time, silence fell between them again until Skye decided to ask Kate another question. "I hope you don't mind my asking, but how did you become a pirate?"

Kate was slow to answer, and her expression became sad as she recalled old and painful memories. Skye was going to be one of the few people ever to hear her story.

"I was a slave all the years of growing up. Ten years ago, when I was about your age, I met another slave named Jim. We planned to escape together and when we were safe . . . we were going to get married. The night of our escape someone betrayed us and told our master what we were doing. Jim was shot as we tried to get away. He insisted that I keep running, so I did."

Kate shook her head as the pain from that night returned. Tears pooled in her dark eyes and her voice quavered a little as she continued. "I never saw him again after that. When I reached the sea, I disguised myself as a man and got a job on a ship, hopin' I could finally be free. I soon found that the captain, a man named Joshua, had also been a slave. When he realized I was a woman, he told me I'd be safe on his ship. He was very kind and a very good friend to me. His crewmen were too. At the time I came to his ship, Joshua was very old and a year later, he died. When he did, he left me the ship and that's how I became the captain of the *Half Moon*."

"I'm sorry about Jim," Skye said after a moment, as her thoughts drifted once again to Will.

Kate nodded. "Would you mind if I asked you a question now?"

"Go ahead," Skye invited.

"Your treasure, is it as big as everyone says?"

Skye nodded. "Yes, it is. My father and Caleb were greatly rewarded for what they did."

"Have you ever thought about what you'd do with it if you were to go and get it?"

"Yes, I have."

"And?"

"Well," Skye began. "I always thought I'd build a bigger church in Kingston so that more people could attend. I'd give a lot of it to the orphanage in hopes that children like me could grow up a little better. And I'd also give some to Will and Matthew."

"Did you ever intend to use any for yourself?"

"Only enough to stop working at the orphanage and try to find and buy back the *Grace*, my father's ship. It was very special to us. He named it after my mother."

Kate nodded again. "Sounds like a good plan."

"Yes, although it all depends on whether or not I actually retrieve the treasure."

"If you get off this island, do you think you will?" Kate asked.

"I don't know," Skye answered. "There's never been anyone who could help me get there."

Before she could say anything else, a tired yawn escaped her.

"You should get some sleep," Kate said. "You have a lot to recover from."

"Are you sure?" Skye asked. "Don't you need help watching the fire?"

Kate shook her head. "I'll put a bunch of wood on it before I go to sleep, and it should stay burnin' 'til morning."

Skye nodded and lay down, careful not to lie on her wound. She closed her eyes, thanked God for getting them safely away from Kelley, and fell into the first peaceful night's sleep she'd had since being kidnapped.

The sun shone down warmly on Skye mid morning of the next day when she began to wake. As the deep, restful sleep slowly wore off, someone called her name. It wasn't until it was spoken a second time that she realized it was not Kate's voice. Her eyes opened instantly, and she sat up. At first, she wondered if she was dreaming.

Chapter Eleven

Will scanned the deck of the *Fortune* and sighed heavily. Since the storm, nearly all daylight hours had been spent making repairs to the ship, though to look at her one would see no progress at all. The knocking of wooden pulleys echoed around him as broken rigging swung uselessly from the masts. One had snapped off during the storm and a torn sail lay in a tattered heap at its base, which was now only a splintered stump.

To make further repairs, John had said they would be able to make it to a port some three or four days away, but that meant temporarily giving up the search for Skye. With the time it was going to take to sail there and repair the ship, a chore that could take another week in itself, Skye could be in Kelley's hands for another two weeks or more. Will was thankful that they had survived the storm, but the thought of what Skye could be going through was more than he could stand, and he was powerless to help her.

Finally, Will turned and headed toward Matthew and John at the helm, but he slowed when he heard an argument brewing between them. John, who was very distraught over the condition of his ship, glared at

Matthew and said, "Oh, and I s'pose you're gonna try to tell me that God even has a plan in all this."

Matthew sighed, not in the mood to go through this again with John. "Yes, John, He has a plan in everything."

"Now why on earth would God allow a storm like that and ruin us?" John demanded.

"I never said I knew the answers to everything." Matthew was trying hard not to get upset. "Some things you never know. But I think you're forgetting that all three of us survived the storm, which you yourself said is a miracle."

"I did not," John retorted with a scowl.

"Before the storm, you said it would take a miracle to keep us afloat and we're still here."

"Well, did you ever consider that maybe God is tryin' to tell you to give up the search?" John questioned. "We've been sailin' around for days, lookin' for one ship in the whole ocean with absolutely no idea where she's headed or how we'll stop Kelley if we do find 'im. Then we come upon this storm that nearly sinks us and it's gonna take the next two weeks before we can actually start searchin' again. Besides, knowin' Kelley, the girl's probably dead anyway."

Will's heart thumped hard in reaction. He could hardly believe that John actually had the audacity to say such a thing. He glared at the pirate and then looked at Matthew who was not pleased with his friend at the moment.

"I will not believe she is dead, John," Matthew told him firmly. "And I don't believe that God is telling us to give up. Whether it takes two weeks, two months, or two years, Will and I are going to keep searching. You can either stop at port, repair the ship, and continue to help us, or drop us off and we'll find someone else who will help."

With these words, Matthew turned away, leaving John to contemplate what he had said. John muttered under his breath, but Will could not make out the words and turned to follow Matthew. As he did so, his eyes caught on the island he had spotted in the distance not too long ago. It was much closer now, and with a second look, Will realized that smoke rose above the trees. He turned back and made his way to John, who looked a little like a pouting child expecting some sort of lecture.

"John, I saw smoke coming from that island."

The expression disappeared as John turned to where Will was pointing. Matthew joined them. John frowned and looped a rope around the wheel before walking to the edge of the ship. He pulled out his spyglass and trained it on the island.

"There's a fire on the beach, all right," he declared.

"Do you see anyone?" Matthew asked.

"No," John answered. He put the spyglass down. "The island's pretty small and looks uninhabited, so it's probably someone who got marooned."

"Shouldn't we help them then?" Will inquired.

John made a face. "I don't know if that's such a wise idea. A lot of men get marooned for betrayin' the rest of the crew."

"Or because the rest of the crew betrayed them," Matthew countered.

John sent him a side-glance. "That's possible. Either way, we may be askin' for trouble. Few would take the chance."

Matthew looked at him, appealing to his humanity. "John, think if it were you. Would you want to be sitting on a beach thinking you were rescued and then have the ship sail off?"

John rolled his eyes. "You just love to make me feel guilty, don't you?"

Matthew grinned slightly. "So you do have a conscience?"

"Yes, I have a conscience," John muttered defensively. "Now quit chitchattin' and help me get this ship closer to the island so we can drop anchor and row ashore."

Will and Matthew traded quick smiles before hurrying to help John move the ship closer to the island. When they were as close as they could get without running aground, they dropped anchor and lowered one of the rowboats into the water. Just before they were going to climb to it, John handed them each a pistol.

"You never know whatcha might find. I say it's best to be prepared."

Will and Matthew took the pistols and climbed down. Several minutes later, they pulled the rowboat onto the beach not far from the fire. Before they had any chance to look around, a woman suddenly emerged from the trees.

"John!" she said in surprise, hurrying toward them.

"Kate!" John echoed, equally surprised. "What on earth are you doin' here? Your crew can't have marooned ya."

Kate shook her head. "No, I wasn't marooned. I was washed overboard durin' the storm along with a friend." Her eyes narrowed questioning, "What are you doin' around here?"

"Well, I've been helpin' these two. We've been searchin' for a girl named—"

"Skye!" Will exclaimed, looking off towards the fire.

Everyone turned as he hurried to where Skye slept beside the fire. Will's breath caught to see the bloodstained rip in the back of Skye's shirt. He knelt down next to her and gently put his hand on her shoulder.

"Skye," he called softly.

She stirred, and he said her name again. This time her eyes opened, and she sat up.

"Will!" she breathed, her eyes wide with shock and joy.

Will helped her up, and Skye immediately put her arms around him, hugging him tightly. He returned the hug, careful not to cause her pain from her injuries.

"I can't believe it's really you," Skye said, letting him go and looking into his face with a smile.

Will looked her over carefully, wanting to know she was all right. He reached up, frowning, and tenderly touched the ends of her short hair.

"Are you all right?" he asked, concern evident in his tone. "What has Kelley done to you?"

Skye's smile diminished a little. "I'm fine, Will. Truly. Kelley could have done a lot worse, but God protected me." She shook her head, almost not believing all of this was true. "How did you find me?"

"I had a lot of help," Will answered, looking off to the side with a smile.

Skye grinned. "Matthew!"

He stepped closer, and Skye gave him a hug as well. After their greeting, Matthew turned to John, who stood close by.

"Skye, I'd like you to meet an old friend of mine, Captain John Morgan," Matthew introduced. "Without him, we wouldn't be here."

John leaned closer to Matthew and murmured, "Oh, so we're friends again now?"

"John," Matthew protested with a sigh.

John finally turned his attention to Skye with a charming smile. "It's a pleasure to meet you, Miss McHenry. Your two friends here have thought of little else on our voyage the past eleven days. They've talked very highly of you, and it's an honor to meet the daughter of Daniel McHenry."

Skye returned his smile. "It's a pleasure to meet you as well, Captain Morgan. Thank you for helping them find me."

She turned back to Will and Matthew. "Now you must meet Kate. She helped me on the *Finder*. God used her greatly in keeping me safe."

Will and Matthew each greeted her warmly and were immensely grateful for her part in aiding Skye. Afterward, John looked at Kate with a deep frown of confusion.

"What were you doin' on the *Finder*?"

"I've been a slave," Kate informed him, her face pinching in disgust. "Kelley captured me at a port nearly a year ago."

"Oh," John said, flustered. "Well, if I, uh, would have known that, maybe I could have . . . um . . . tried to do somethin'."

Kate shook her head to relieve his discomfort. "Your ship is a lot smaller than the *Finder*, John. I don't think there was anything you could've done."

John only shrugged. "Still, I coulda tried."

He just stood quiet for a moment, but then turned to Matthew and Will with a grin and said, "Well, I don't know about you two, but I say we get these two charmin' women off this island and back to the *Fortune*."

"Good idea," Will agreed.

After gathering a good amount of fruit to take with, the five of them climbed into the boat and rowed toward the ship. As they drew near, Kate observed its sorry condition.

"Looks like you had a rough time durin' the storm too," she remarked.

John nodded. That's when Kate realized she saw no one on board the ship.

"John, where's your crew?"

"Don't have one," John answered simply.

"You mean it's only the three of you?" Kate asked in disbelief.

"Only the three of us," John repeated.

"What happened to your crew?"

"Well, let's just say when I mentioned we were goin' after Kelley, they had some loyalty issues and decided that Tortuga was a little safer."

"I see," Kate said. "So just how did the three of you manage to survive the storm?"

Before he could answer, John caught Matthew giving him a look and refrained from using the smart-aleck remark he was forming in his mind.

"Why don't you ask my friends?" he suggested finally, glowering at Matthew.

"God protected us," Will spoke up confidently.

Kate nodded thoughtfully, and they were all silent until they reached the ship. One by one, they climbed aboard. The men pulled the boat up and made ready to hoist the anchor and set sail.

As John walked near, Kate stopped him. "John, do you have extra clothes that Skye and I can change into?"

"I don't have any dresses if that's whatcha mean," John answered.

Kate crossed her arms, eyes flashing with irritation. "Since when have you ever seen me wear a dress?"

Immediately realizing that he was treading on dangerous ground, John quickly raised his hands in submission. "Never. My mistake. There should be a trunk full of clothes below deck."

"Good, now what about bandages and medical supplies?" Kate wanted to know. "Skye has a wound that should be taken care of."

"There's a cabinet near the galley that I was luckily able to fill just recently," John told her without a moment's hesitation.

Kate nodded in approval and told Skye to follow her below. John watched them go before turning to take the wheel, but found himself instead face to face with Will and Matthew. By the way Matthew was looking at him, John could tell he was amused by something.

John frowned at him. "What is that look s'posed ta mean?"

"I was just wondering something," Matthew said, careful to keep his face straight.

"Wonderin' what?" John wanted to know as he made his way past him.

"Backing down so quickly with Kate, was it out of respect or . . . love?"

John spun around and looked at Matthew as if he were completely insane. "What?"

"I wanted to know if it was out of respect or—"

"I heard what you said. I want to know what it was s'posed ta mean."

"I was just wondering if you have feelings for Kate," Matthew said more plainly. "You did, after all, say that if you had known she was on the *Finder*, you would have done something."

"Nonsense," John insisted, though Will could easily see he was blushing. He turned quickly to go about his work and muttered, "You're crazy."

Matthew smiled at Will as they followed after John.

Chapter Twelve

Below deck, Skye and Kate came to a large trunk. Kate lifted the lid, revealing a disorganized heap of clothes.

"Help yourself," Kate told her.

The two of them searched through the trunk for clothing that would fit their smaller builds. As she pulled out a few shirts to look at, Kate glanced at Skye with a smile.

"Last night when I asked you about your friends, I never imagined I'd get to meet 'em, especially so soon," she remarked.

Skye's face lit with a smile as well. "I know. I couldn't have been more stunned or overjoyed to wake up and see Will."

"He's a very nice young man," Kate commented.

"Yes, he is. The nicest I have ever met." Skye paused with an adoring look.

Kate grinned and teased, "Handsome too."

Skye blushed and was silent for a long moment before saying, "I was so afraid I'd never see him again."

Skye turned her attention back to the trunk. Before long, she had picked out a pair of dark breeches and a white shirt like those she had on, but clean and much nicer. She also pulled out a brown waistcoat.

When Kate had found what she wanted, she went to the cabinet John had told her about and gathered bandages and some ointment, all items that pirates rarely came by. She and Skye then changed into the new clothes and Kate tended Skye's wound.

"Thank you, Kate," Skye said when she finished.

Kate smiled as they left the cabin. "You're welcome.

On deck, Skye knew that Will and Matthew were very anxious to hear the tale she had to tell them. She and Kate walked up to the helm where the two of them waited with John and Skye took a seat on a barrel that Will pulled up for her. From there, she told them everything that had happened since the night she was taken from the orphanage. When Skye came to the part about the storm saving her from being beaten by Kelley, Matthew glanced momentarily at John, who squirmed a little under his friend's gaze. God had used the storm for His plan.

As soon as all the stories had been told, Will and Matthew stood to get back to the ship repairs they had been doing early that morning. Skye and Kate helped as well, though Skye was limited as to what she could do without causing herself pain. Will kept a close watch on her and quickly came to her aid whenever she needed it.

Some time later, John grew tired of standing at the wheel, watching the work, so he called, "Who wants to take over up here for a while?"

"I can."

John was a little surprised to see Skye. She walked up beside him, ready and eager to take the responsibility of steering the ship.

"Do you think you can handle it?" John asked after studying her for a moment.

Skye only nodded.

John stepped back, letting her take the wheel, though she could sense his reluctance.

"Just keep 'er goin' straight east, all right?" he said. His tone made it obvious he was not quite comfortable giving up his place to her, by no means wanting to end up going in the wrong direction.

Skye nodded again and grinned ever so slightly. "Toward Puerto Seguro, right?"

John's look of shock was a bit comical. "Whoever told you that? I never even told Matthew and Will where we were headed."

"Well, you need a port where you can make repairs that's also a safe haven for pirates, and Puerto Seguro is the closest one," Skye deduced simply, the little grin never leaving her face.

Clever girl, John thought to himself. He nodded. "Yes, Miss McHenry, you're right. We are headed for Puerto Seguro, so steer us in that direction."

Skye nodded, then said, "One more thing. Please call me Skye."

"All right, Skye," John replied with a smile before he walked away to join the others.

Standing at the helm reminded Skye how much she had loved it the few times her father had allowed her to take the wheel. She had been so young then, and she wondered what her father would think if he could see her now as a young woman instead of a little girl. She hoped with all her heart that he would be proud of her.

For the rest of the afternoon and into the evening, Skye took turns with Kate steering the ship while the men worked. When darkness crept over the ship, John called the repairs to a halt. As he headed toward the wheel to take over again for Skye, Matthew stopped him for a moment.

"John, will you please tell Skye that I would like to talk to her?"

"Of course," John answered.

He continued on his way until he stopped next to Skye at the wheel.

"Well, you've kept us on a very straight course today. Good job," he told her.

Skye smiled. "Thank you."

As John took the wheel, Skye stepped away, headed down to the galley to help Kate, who was preparing supper for everyone. John, however, informed her of Matthew's desire to speak with her. Skye thanked him once again and walked over to Matthew where they talked quietly as they went below deck.

A moment later, John spotted Will slowly making his way toward the helm. He either had nothing else to do or was too fixed on what was in his mind to make any conscious decision about where he was going. When Will stopped by his side, John smirked, willing to bet anything he had on what he figured the young man was thinking about. He grinned slyly as he glanced at Will before looking back out at the sea.

"Is Matthew tellin' her that he's a McHenry?" John asked after a moment. He wondered if he should carry out a little friendly teasing or not.

Will nodded. "How long have you known?"

"Just since he told me the other day."

"You didn't learn his last name when he helped you?"

John shrugged. "Can't remember. Even if I did, the name McHenry didn't have any meanin' back then, so it's no surprise that I forgot."

Still staring straight ahead, John finally decided that instead of getting around to what he wanted to know by teasing Will, he'd just ask the question straight out. *You're gonna sound just like Matthew,* he told himself, but, at the moment, he didn't really care.

After a long silence he asked suddenly, "You love her, don't you?"

Will turned to him in surprise. Before he could even think of how to reply, John spoke again.

"Any idiot could see you have feelings for her just by the way you look at her, so you might as well just admit it."

Will was still surprised by John's bluntness, but he nodded and said, "You're right; I do have feelings for her, and I would never deny it."

John nodded in approval and asked, "How long have you had 'em?"

"For as long as I can remember," Will answered.

John abandoned all thoughts of teasing. "Have you ever told her that?"

Will lowered his head and shook it. He truly had meant to. "Not yet."

John turned to him while still keeping a hand on the wheel. "You may not think of me as the best candidate to be givin' advice about this sorta thing, but if I were you, I'd tell her soon. You never know when a time could come when you realize you've lost your chance."

Will thought about John's words. He was right, and Will had already told himself the very same thing many times before. Only now, since Skye had been kidnapped, did he realize how very true the words were. He couldn't bear the thought of how horribly close Skye had come to never knowing that he loved her.

Before John could speak again, a smile spread across Will's face, and he just couldn't resist asking, "Have you told Kate yet?"

John rolled his eyes. His former plan of teasing had backfired on him. "This has nothin' to do with Kate," he said in annoyance. Still, he couldn't help but silently congratulate Will for such a clever response. It was exactly what he would have said if he had been in Will's position. Speaking again with no trace of annoyance in his voice, John continued, "This is about you and Skye. You've got a special girl there, and I wouldn't risk never gettin' to tell her how I felt."

Will smiled and nodded. "I will tell her." He paused. "But not tonight."

John looked at him for an explanation.

"Tonight I'll just let her enjoy what Matthew has told her," Will decided. "I think she's already had quite an overwhelming day and doesn't need anything else to think about."

John agreed. "Good idea."

With nothing more to be said, Will walked away toward the stairs that led below deck. He descended them just in time to see Skye lean over with a big smile on her face and hug Matthew. Will smiled as well. He loved to see Skye so happy.

Kate walked in from the galley a moment later. "I'm sorry if I'm interruptin'," she said apologetically, "but the food is ready."

As he and Skye approached Kate, Matthew thanked her for preparing their meal. "I'll go take the wheel for John. He can eat first," he told her.

Kate nodded and returned to the galley as Matthew went up to get John, leaving Skye and Will alone. Skye smiled at him, her blue eyes sparkling like sapphires.

"Did Matthew tell you?" she asked.

"Yes," Will answered, his smile equally joyful.

"I'm still in shock," Skye said, shaking her head as she remembered what had taken place only moments ago.

"I know. It shocked me too," Will admitted. "It was the last thing I ever expected."

"I should have known though," Skye realized. "I've always thought he seemed so much like my father." She smiled again. "I feel so happy right now. I finally have family, at least family I can be close to."

"I'm very happy for you," Will told her. "I know how much you've longed for that."

A moment of contented silence fell between them, in which they only smiled at each other. Eyes running over her upturned face, Will wanted so badly to tell Skye how much he cared for her, how much he loved her, but he cared too greatly to risk ruining one of the happiest moments of her life, even in some small way.

The silence was broken by movement above them as John came down the stairs. When he saw them, he hesitated.

"Excuse me if I'm interruptin' anything," he said, wondering if perhaps Will had changed his mind about what he had said.

"We were just talking about Matthew," Will assured him.

When John heard that, he continued the rest of the way down the stairs and smiled at Skye.

"Well, you've had a very surprisin' day, haven't you?" he remarked. "First you wake up to see him," he gestured at Will, "and then you find out that Matthew's your uncle."

Skye nodded with a blissful smile. "Yes, it truly has been one of the most surprising—as well as the happiest—days of my life."

Chapter Thirteen

Late in the evening, three days after Skye and Kate had been rescued from the island, John expertly navigated the *Fortune* into the sheltered bay of Puerto Seguro. During the voyage, Will had been thinking constantly about the advice John had given him. He had been intent on telling Skye how he felt and had tried several times, but each time there had been an interruption. It really wasn't anyone's fault. There wasn't much privacy on a ship, even if it was just the five of them, and Will was never alone with Skye long enough to say what he wanted to say.

Will and Skye stood side by side at the bow of the ship now as John prepared to drop anchor. They looked at the town spread before them. Its weathered wooden buildings sat haphazardly along a beach scattered with nets, crates, and other signs of human habitation. The white forms of gulls dotted the beach as they looked for dead fish and other food that had been left behind. Puerto Seguro looked a lot like Tortuga, though it was only about half the size. Several pirate ships of notable reputation were already anchored alongside the numerous docks.

"Did you ever come here with your father?" Will asked, looking at Skye.

"Once or twice, but I never went into town. I rarely did, being so young. These ports are, after all, pirate settlements." Making a face, she continued, "You know what Tortuga is like. Places like these are not much different."

Will agreed that they weren't good places for anyone, least of all children as young as she had been.

John gave the order to drop anchor. When it had been lowered, everyone helped moor the ship to the dock before going ashore. Once they had reached the beach, John turned to Matthew, and Skye and Will.

"I imagine you three aren't gonna want to stick around here for the next week while I'm havin' repairs done to the ship, so if ya'd like, I could help you find someone to take you back to Kingston," John offered. "Or at least somewhere close by."

Matthew smiled. "Thank you, John. We'd appreciate that."

"Follow me," John said as he walked down the beach, looking at every anchored ship they passed. Speaking mostly to himself, he continued, "There must be someone here I can trust to get my friends back to safety."

Having passed by a good five or more, John abruptly stopped.

"Perfect," he said in satisfaction as he grinned at one ship.

"What is this ship?" Skye asked.

"The *Sea Devil*," Kate answered.

"The *Sea Devil*?" Will repeated skeptically.

John turned to him. "She ain't the prettiest name, I'll give you that, but her captain is the second most trustworthy pirate you'll find anywhere. He's the only one I'd trust to take you three back to Kingston."

Matthew looked at him quizzically. "John, if he's the second most trustworthy pirate, who's the first?"

John's grin widened. "You're lookin' at 'im."

Kate raised her eyebrows. "And where exactly does that leave me, Captain Morgan?"

"Ah, well . . . I seem to have made a little mistake," John replied quickly. "What I meant was he's the third, *you're* the first, and I'm the second."

A smile of approval came to Kate's face, and Skye and Will could not help laughing.

"And just what do you two find so funny?" John wanted to know.

"I didn't know pirates could be considered trustworthy," Will confessed.

"Well now, that's just a matter of opinion." John looked at Skye. "You considered your father trustworthy, right?"

"Of course."

"Would you even have considered him trustworthy when he sailed for Kelley?"

"Yes."

"And now I'm sure you consider Kate here to be trustworthy."

Skye nodded.

John looked again at Will with a grin. "Ya see, pirates can be considered trustworthy." He continued toward the *Sea Devil*, leaving everyone else to follow behind. "Now, if *I* were not trustworthy, I might have decided that treasure of Skye's was a little too temptin' and tried to find out where it is myself, but I didn't. Then, I could have decided that searchin' for Skye was just a waste of time, which it wasn't, and just thrown Matthew and Will off at some port with no way to get home . . . "

John would have rattled off a dozen other things to prove his trustworthiness, but they had reached the dock where the *Sea Devil* was anchored. A few feet in front of John, a young man worked on some rigging.

"Excuse me, lad, is this ship still captained by Abe Foley?" John asked.

"Aye, sir, she is," the young man answered.

"Is he aboard?"

"Aye."

John grinned. "Good. Go tell 'im that John Morgan's here to see 'im."

The young man nodded and boarded the ship while John and the others waited on the dock. Within the space of a minute, a man appeared on the deck of the ship and peered down at them from over the rail. He was short, heavyset, about sixty-five years old, and had a thick gray beard and hair.

"John!" he exclaimed, grinning broadly.

"Hello, Abe," John called.

"What brings ya to Puerto Seguro?" Abe asked.

"My ship is in bad need of repairs after that storm a few days ago. And now that I've found you, I wanna ask you to do a favor for me," John declared.

"Come aboard so we can talk," Abe invited. "Bring yer friends with ya."

He walked away from the railing and disappeared from sight.

John motioned for everyone to follow him up the gangplank and onto the *Sea Devil* where Abe was waiting. When they reached the other captain, he took John's hand with a grin and shook it heartily. "It's mighty good to see ya again, John." He then turned to Kate and shook her hand too, "And Kate, it's good to see you again too."

"It's good to see you, too, Abe. It's been awhile," Kate said with a smile.

Abe looked around. "Did ya both bring yer ships here? Where's Riley and the rest of yer crew, Kate?"

"Actually, Abe," John began slowly, "it's only the five of us and the *Fortune*." He knew now he would never be able to leave the ship without telling Abe *everything*.

"Just the five of ya and the *Fortune*," Abe repeated, frowning. "What happened?"

"It's a *long* story," John told him, hoping the emphasis on *long* might discourage Abe from wanting to hear it.

"I've got time," Abe said. "Why don'tcha come to my cabin and you can tell me all about it."

Before John could accept or decline the invitation, Abe turned and headed for the cabin. *That's Abe*, John thought. He again motioned for the others to follow. Inside the large cabin, Abe told everyone to sit down around a table. Taking his own seat, he looked closely at Skye, Will, and Matthew.

"Who are yer friends, John?"

John introduced them each in turn. "Abe, this is Skylar McHenry, William James, and Matthew McHenry."

"Skylar McHenry," Abe said, looking at her in surprise. "Ya wouldn't happen to be the child of Daniel McHenry, would ya?"

"Yes, I am," Skye replied.

"Well now, I never thought I'd live to see the day when I'd get to meet another McHenry, 'specially the daughter of old Daniel," Abe said with a grin. "It's a pleasure to meetcha, darlin'. Yer father was a great man and though most of us were afeared of 'im, we had a lotta respect for 'im too."

Skye smiled and Abe turned his gaze to Matthew. "So yer a McHenry too? Are ya related to Daniel?"

Matthew nodded. "I'm his younger brother."

"I didn't know 'e had any kin," Abe said in interest.

"We were separated in England when our parents died, and I never got the chance to see him again before . . . before he died."

Abe shook his head with regret. "It's a real shame. The world needs more men like 'im, 'im and that friend of 'is."

"Caleb," Skye murmured quietly, still able to see his kind, fun-loving light blue eyes.

Abe nodded. After a silent moment of remorse, he looked at Will. "So, lad, who might you be to Mr. and Miss McHenry?"

"Skye and I grew up together at the orphanage in Kingston," Will told him.

"Good friends then, I'll bet," Abe said.

Will nodded. "Yes." *And more*, he thought, his mind going back to the fact that he still hadn't told Skye he loved her.

Abe nodded in approval. "Good. A person always needs some good friends, ain't that right, John?"

"Always," John agreed.

"So now, tell me, John, how did ya come to have Kate and the last two survivin' McHenry's all on the *Fortune?*"

John knew getting out of telling the story would be impossible, so he began. A half an hour later, Abe's curiosity and questions were finally satisfied. He looked at Skye.

"You've had quite a rough time, haven'tcha, Miss McHenry?"

"Yes," Skye answered, "though it could have been worse."

"That it could have," Abe agreed. "I bet yer anxious to get it all behind ya."

Skye nodded.

"That brings me to the favor I need to ask you," John told Abe. "It's gonna take at least a week to get the *Fortune* back into good sailin' condition— "

"Oh, it'll take longer than that," Abe interrupted. "Since that storm, Puerto Seguro's been picked clean of repairin' materials, as well as supplies like food and water. I got the last of it two days ago. Yer gonna have ta wait for the next supply ship ta come through."

"Well then, that makes the favor even more important," John said. "Ya see, I don't want my friends to have to wait here in Puerto Seguro all that time while I get the *Fortune* repaired and you're the only one I'd trust to take 'em safely to Kingston. What do ya say, Abe?" He fixed Abe with a persuasive grin. "Will you do an old friend a favor and take his friends safely back home?"

Abe thought it over. "Kingston, ya say?"

John nodded.

"Well, it's a little outta the way, and I can't very well go sailin' into the port, but for you and the memory of old Daniel, I'll get 'em as close as I can," Abe decided.

John smiled. "Thanks, Abe. I knew I could count on ya."

Skye, Will, and Matthew thanked him as well.

"When will you be sailin'?" John asked.

"I plan to weigh anchor at dawn."

"We'll be here," Matthew told him.

Abe nodded. They said their goodbyes then, and John led them off the ship. Back on the beach, John suddenly slowed and turned to Matthew.

"Well, I guess we'll soon be sayin' goodbye and who knows if our paths will ever cross again," he said with more than a bit of remorse. "That bein' the case, there's somethin' I've been meanin' to tell you, and I'd better just come out with it."

"What is it, John?" Matthew asked.

"Well . . . " John shifted around nervously. "It's about when I was criticizin' what you believe the day we rescued Kate and Skye. I didn't mean . . . um . . . I guess I was just kinda upset about the *Fortune* and I, uh . . . "

Matthew smiled and put his hand on John's shoulder. "Apology accepted."

John grinned. "Oh good, now that that's behind us, what do ya say to goin' and havin' our last meal all together. I know a place that has some great food and drinks . . . that is, if you don't mind."

Matthew nodded. "As long as you keep them at a limit. I'd hate to spend our last night carrying you back to the *Fortune* so drunk you don't recognize me again."

John laughed. "You've got yourself a deal."

He led them into the small, bustling town. They shortly came to an old tavern that looked like it had not seen any repairs in years. Skye looked up at the sign above the door. She thought she made out part of the words *gold* and possibly *lady*, but the rest of the paint was so chipped she could not read anything else.

"This is it," John said with a grin. "Pay no heed to the outside, it's much better inside."

They followed him through the door and were immediately greeted by the strong smell of alcohol from the rum and ale served at the bar. The large room was filled with men sitting at round tables, talking loudly with the bar girls. Seeing them reminded Skye precisely of why she had never gone into many of the towns with her father, though this place wasn't as bad as some she had seen and heard of.

Over the clamor of noise, a voice boomed out from the bar.

"Can it really be Captain John Morgan?"

John winced noticeably and turned toward the bar where a giant of a man stood. His height exceeded Will and Matthew's by at least a whole head.

"Hello, David," John greeted the barkeeper with a forced smile.

"What can I do for you?" David asked.

"I want your finest for me an' my friends here," John instructed.

"Drinks too?"

"Just for me . . . " He looked at Kate.

"One," she told him.

" . . . and one for Kate."

"Only one?" David inquired.

"You heard 'im, David," Kate spoke up.

"Aye, one," David repeated.

He turned to get the food, and John led everyone over to an empty table at the far side of the room. They sat around it and waited, talking amongst themselves in the sea of chaos. A few minutes later, David brought them a large tray of food and several mugs of rum, one for Kate and the rest for John. They began eating and found, as John had promised, the food to be very good. Having grown tired of the little they could make on the ship, they all enjoyed it.

129

When she had finished her portion, Kate stood. "If you'll all excuse me, I'm gonna find out if anyone's seen the *Half Moon* lately and spread the word that if someone does see 'em to tell 'em that Captain's lookin' for 'em."

John nodded, wanting her to get back to her ship as much as she did. "Good idea. And we'll make sure you don't go an' disappear on us."

Kate grinned at him and then crossed the room to a table where a few pirates she obviously was acquainted with sat. She had barely left when David called out to their little table again.

"Hey, John, why don'tcha come up here and tell me the goings on with you lately?"

John sighed heavily and looked at Matthew. "He's gonna be askin' me that all night if I don't go up there. He's the kind who can't keep 'is nose out of other peoples' business. He's gotta know everything."

Matthew found himself laughing at the sour look on John's face. "Go up and talk to him while the three of us finish eating," he proposed.

"You sure?" John asked, hesitant to leave them.

Matthew nodded and John rose from the table.

"I'll try not to be too long," John told them, though he didn't sound optimistic.

He left them to finish their meal, approaching the bar with great reluctance.

Twenty minutes crept past and John still stood at the bar with no sign of his conversation with David abating. The three of them waited at the table, watching him hopefully. For Skye, the crowdedness of the tavern, the ungodly behavior, and the smell of alcohol was starting to get very stifling.

To make matters worse, Will and Matthew had to occasionally shoo away bar girls who neither seemed to understand nor care that they were not wanted. What bothered Will even more was that Skye had a few of the drunken pirates showing some interest in her as well. Skye was thankful to have Will and Matthew right there to keep them away, but the whole situation was becoming increasingly uncomfortable. Will and Skye were very relieved when Matthew quite suddenly stood up to say, "Let's go back to the *Fortune* and wait for John and Kate there."

Eager to go along with the idea, Will and Skye followed Matthew to the bar. John turned slightly when Matthew tapped him on the shoulder, still trying to look like he was listening to David, who seemed not to notice that John's full attention was no longer on him.

"We're going back to the *Fortune*," Matthew murmured.

"I'll be along as soon as I can," John said, sighing and turning back to David, who was still oblivious to anything but his own voice.

Matthew nodded and they walked out of the tavern. Outside, Skye took a long, deep breath of the fresh sea air and sighed with relief. She heard Will do the same.

"I'll be glad never to visit a place like that again," Skye announced as they headed through the dark, empty streets towards the bay.

"You and me both," Will responded with feeling.

"They are not pleasant places," Matthew agreed.

They were halfway to the docks when three dark figures appeared on the street. Skye, Will, and Matthew came to an abrupt halt. The men wore dark clothing and their faces were covered.

131

"If you men are looking for money, we have very little with us. Certainly not enough to fight over," Matthew told them as he rested his hand on the hilt of his sword.

The man in the middle stepped forward and his cruel, harsh laugh penetrated the dark silence. Reaching up, he pulled back the covering from his face. Skye gasped and fear raced through her body.

"On the contrary, you have something very valuable." He peered at Skye. "Good evening, Miss McHenry. What a pleasant surprise it is to see you alive and well. I thought you had drowned during the storm, which would have been a most unfortunate event. How lucky it is for me to have met up with you here."

With those words, Will and Matthew knew exactly who he was. Francis Kelley.

Still speaking to Skye, Kelley said, "Now why don't you just come along with me quietly and yer friends can go on their way."

Matthew and Will pulled out their swords before Skye could speak. Will stepped slightly in front of her, ready to defend her with his life.

"You won't take her again, Kelley," he declared.

Kelley smirked. "I do believe that is up to Miss McHenry."

Skye stared at Kelley for a moment and then pulled out the sword John had given her before they went ashore. She would not be Kelley's prisoner again.

Kelley chuckled. "So that's the way you want to do this, is it?"

Before anyone could make a move, Skye heard the click of a pistol hammer being pulled back, and Will stiffened. Startled, Skye turned to see something that

132

made her heart skip a beat. A pirate stood behind them with a pistol pressed to the back of Will's head. He was joined by several more pirates appearing from the shadows until they were surrounded.

"What do you say now, Miss McHenry?" Kelley asked with an evil grin.

With a horrible sinking feeling, Skye could only let her sword slip from her hand, not willing to jeopardize Will's safety. Matthew did the same. Will, however, held on to his as he stared at Kelley, devastated by the fact that he could do nothing to stop Skye from being taken into this evil man's hands once again. Kelley looked at him scornfully.

"Don't try to be a hero, boy. You'd be dead before you could even make a move."

Having no other choice, Will finally let his sword slip through his fingers.

Chapter Fourteen

Finally!" John sighed heavily as he and Kate walked out of the tavern nearly an hour and a half later. "He just can't shut up, can 'e? I thought we'd never get outta there. Matthew, Skye, and Will must be sleepin' by now."

Kate laughed. "You never were very good at tellin' people you had to go."

John scoffed. "As if sayin' it about six dozen times ain't enough."

Kate laughed again. "Well, at least we're out of there now, so let's hurry back to the *Fortune* before David realizes there's somethin' he forgot to ask you and tries to find us."

John rolled his eyes and muttered, "He'd better not or I just might put a permanent end to that blabberin' of his."

"John," Kate scolded as she reached out and smacked him on the arm.

"I was only sayin' it," John told her. He grinned devilishly, causing Kate to laugh again.

Chuckling together, they continued toward the *Fortune*. When they reached the docks, John frowned at the darkened ship.

"Now why didn't they leave a lantern burnin' for us?" he wondered.

"Maybe they did and it went out," Kate suggested.

With an unexplained feeling of apprehension, John made his way up the gangplank and onto the ship's deck. Hair prickled on the back of his neck right before he came to a sudden stop and stared wide-eyed at the mainmast in front of him. Matthew, Skye, and Will were each bound to it and gagged.

Before his mind could even begin to process why they were there, something moved behind him and Kate gasped. He pulled out his sword as he spun around. An unfamiliar pirate had his dagger up to Kate's throat. Footsteps thudded on deck. Looking off to his right, John spotted several more pirates. Immediately, he recognized the one in front and glared with hatred as the man spoke.

"Well, now, if it isn't Captain John Morgan, the man who was once foolish enough to attempt to kill me. I thought for sure you were dead," Kelley said with disappointment.

"And if it isn't Francis Kelley, the man who murdered my best friend and first mate," John retorted bitterly. "Trust me, I'd never give you of all people the satisfaction of knowin' you'd killed me."

"Still as spiteful as ever, ain't ya?"

"Give me one good reason I shouldn't be."

"We're pirates, John," Kelley reminded him. "We don't have friends and killin' is what we're known for."

"It's what you're known for Kelley, not me," John shot back. "And I do have friends, which is somethin' you'll surely never have, so I consider myself highly fortunate."

Kelley shook his head. "We can stand here exchangin' words all night, John, but I'm not that patient. Now drop yer sword," he demanded.

"Or what, Kelley? You'll just shoot me again, like the coward you are?"

Kelley narrowed his eyes. "If you value her health, John . . . ," he gestured at Kate, ". . . which I really believe you do, you'd be wise not to upset me."

Glancing at Kate, who drew in her breath as the dagger was pressed threateningly against her throat, John sighed in disgust. He tossed his sword toward Kelley.

"Happy?" he said with a counterfeit smile that reflected his loathing for the other pirate captain.

"Quite," Kelley replied smugly. He turned to the other pirates. "Bind their hands."

Once John and Kate's hands were tied securely, Kelley stepped closer to John now that he was bound and unarmed.

"I'm sure you, like me, have heard that there's no supplies left here, which presents a bit of a problem. How much food and water do you have in yer hold?"

John smirked. "Why don't you go look?"

Kelley glared at him. "This is yer second warnin', John. There'd better not be a third." He turned to some of his men. "Go see how much he has for supplies in the hold."

Two of the men hurried below deck. They returned a couple of minutes later and reported, "There's enough for a coupla days."

Kelley nodded in satisfaction. "That'll be just enough to reach Malvado. We'll get the rest of what we need there. Take everything useful over to the *Finder*. When

136

you're done . . . ," he paused, glancing at John, ". . . burn the ship."

John narrowed his eyes. "You wouldn't dare."

Kelley ignored him and turned to the rest of his men. "Take the prisoners to the ship."

The pirates cut Skye, Will, and Matthew free of the mast and all five were paraded off the *Fortune*, down the beach to where the *Finder* was anchored at the opposite side of the bay. Once aboard the dark, foreboding ship, Kelley had everyone tied to the railing where they would be out of the way, but he could still keep an eye on them. For a long time, Kelley's men carried supplies from the *Fortune* to the *Finder*. Nearly an hour later, one of the men finally returned to Kelley and said, "That's the last of it, Captain. They're preparin' to set the ship afire now."

Kelley grinned victoriously and strode over to John, who was quite horrified at what they were about to do to his ship. Draping his arm around John's shoulders, as though they were old friends, Kelley pointed toward the *Fortune*.

"You should be seein' flames any moment now," he said, the cruel, arrogant grin never leaving his face.

John angrily shrugged him off and did not reply, his gaze trained on his ship. It was not but a few seconds before bright orange flames leapt up from the *Fortune's* deck. The flames crept up the masts and devoured what sails the pirates had left behind. Soon, the ship was nothing more than a burning piece of wreckage. The two pirates who had lit the fire returned shortly, laughing between themselves, their evil mockery tearing at John's heart. Kelley turned to join them and praise their work, but John's words brought him to an immediate halt.

"You won't get away with this," John warned, breathing heavily. "You won't get away with what you intend to do to us or what you did to Nathan either."

Kelley shook his head in annoyance. "For your sake, John, forget about Nathan. It was a long time ago. You can't hold onto the past forever."

John glared murderously at him. "I will *never* forget about 'im, and I'll make sure you don't either."

Kelley returned the intense glare. "You try anything and I'll see to it that you end up the same way you did then, lyin' on a beach with a bullet in yer chest. But this time, I'll make sure you're dead."

With those words, Kelley stalked off and gave orders to his crew.

"It's time to set sail before someone gets it into their head to be noble and tries to stop us. Weigh anchor and set course for Malvado. Take the prisoners below deck. Put the women in one cell and the men in another."

Skye and the others were cut from the railing and forced below. Skye's hands were untied and the gag was taken from her mouth after having been nearly choking her for the past couple hours. The pirates shoved her into a cell with Kate while Will, Matthew, and John were pushed into one next to it. When the pirates had gone, John looked at each of them.

"Is everyone all right?"

They nodded, their faces grim. John turned to Matthew with sorrowful bewilderment. "What happened?"

Matthew exhaled loudly. "We were on our way to the *Fortune* when Kelley stopped us in the street. He wanted Skye. We thought it was only him and two others so we were prepared to fight, but another man snuck up behind Will with a pistol. We were surrounded and had no choice but to surrender."

"Sounds like 'e had it all planned, but how did 'e know Skye was here?"

"His men must have seen us in the tavern. He knew you and Kate were there. That's why he took us to the *Fortune* instead of just coming straight here to the *Finder*," Matthew explained. "He didn't want to leave without securing the two of you as well."

John shook his head and muttered, "The dirty . . . " Several words came to mind. He did not feel right saying them in front of Matthew or Skye and Will, so instead he just fell silent. Matthew was the one who finally broke that silence.

"John, when we were in Tortuga, why didn't you tell us you knew Kelley? And who is Nathan?"

John sighed. "I didn't say anything because I didn't want to be asked any questions."

"I see," Matthew said sympathetically. "I am sorry."

John shook his head. "Nah, don't be. I was just bein' a fool and tryin' to act like I didn't really care about anything." He sat down heavily against the bars of the cell. Everyone else sat as well, keeping intent eyes on him. "Nathan was my truest friend before I met you, Matthew. About three years before you saved me, Nathan and I were crewmen here on the *Finder*."

Everyone was surprised by this news, but not wishing to interrupt, they said nothing. "At that time, we thought Kelley's bloodthirsty reputation was just some story to frighten people, but of course, we soon found out how wrong we were.

"The next time we made port, Nathan and I took our share of what treasure we had collected and left without informin' Kelley. We used our money and bought our own little ship. I was the captain and Nathan was my first mate. We only took from Kelley what we were owed, but he still came after us.

"Nathan and I managed to stay one step ahead of him for about a year and a half, but then he caught us when we stopped at a port. He demanded that we give back what we took as well as more for the trouble we'd caused. He and I started to argue and things got a little rough so Nathan spoke up, tryin' to defend me. Without warning, Kelley pulled out his pistol and shot him dead, right there.

"Kelley and I fought then. I, of course, had every intention of killin' 'im, but he grabbed another pistol from one of his men and shot me. He left me to die on the beach. I thought for sure I was done for, but I woke up three days later in the house of the local doctor who had found me and was kind enough to help me. He patched me up and I lived. I wish the same could've been said for Nathan." John shook his head. "Kelley had no call to kill 'im."

"I'm sorry, John," Matthew consoled his friend.

Everyone else offered their condolences and he thanked them for their sympathies but then changed the subject to something that was of dire importance, their escape from the ship. They discussed their options, which were pitiful at best, and it only led them to the undeniable realization of why Kate had tried for nearly a year to get off the ship without success. It was nearly impossible. How could all five of them get off when Kelley would surely be keeping an especially close watch on Skye?

Still, they continued trying to come up with a plan. Meanwhile, Skye silently prayed to God for His help. He had provided a way for her and Kate off the *Finder* once, and she prayed that He would do it again for all of them. Catching a few of Will's glances, Skye knew he was doing the same. It was easy to see how worried he was for her. Every one of them knew that because Skye had escaped Kelley once, he would now be especially desperate to find out the location of the treasure.

Finally, miserable with exhaustion, they gave up and fell silent. It was already well past midnight, and they had worn themselves out. In spite of her worries, Skye found herself being lulled to sleep by the sound of waves.

Chapter Fifteen

Skye woke with a start in the early dawn to the familiar and dreaded sound of footsteps approaching the cells. Everyone pushed themselves up with audible sighs and signs of weariness. Kelley and a couple of his men appeared, looking especially pleased with themselves. He stopped between the two cells and glanced at each of them with a self-satisfied grin.

"How is everyone this fine mornin'?" he taunted.

"Oh, we're just dandy," John replied, his voice full of sarcasm. "Why don't you come in here an' join us?" If only he could get his hands on the hateful man.

Kelley chuckled, in far too good a mood for John's words to anger him. He stepped closer to the cell. It had been too late the night before to ask Skye's two friends any questions, but he intended to do so now. His eyes rested first on Will. Clearly the young man cared a great deal for Skye by the way he had stepped up, trying to protect her, and his reluctance to drop his sword when everyone else had. *He may be useful*, Kelley thought. *Or troublesome*.

"You, what is yer name?" Kelley asked him.

Will stared at him for only a short moment and looked away. He had no intention of answering. Kelley's face hardened with irritation.

"Don't be stubborn with me, boy," he warned. "If I have to force you to tell me, I promise it will be anythin' but pleasant."

Kelley's words frightened Skye. She could not bear the thought of him hurting Will. Will saw fear in her expression and sighed. His eyes dug deeply into Skye's as he answered, "William."

"And yer last name?"

Will hesitated again, but then answered. "James."

"Well, welcome aboard the *Finder*, William James," Kelley said with a grin of satisfaction. He stared at Will for a few seconds more. *He's a stubborn one, but I'll bet one threat against the girl will make him as obedient as a trained dog.* Still grinning over these thoughts, Kelley turned his gaze to Matthew. "And just what is yer name?"

"Matthew."

Kelley rolled his eyes. "When I ask for a name, I want the whole name, first and last."

"My name is Matthew McHenry."

Kelley peered at him. "Matthew McHenry," he repeated. "Is that a strange coincidence or are you of any relation to Daniel?"

"I'm his brother."

Kelley grinned again. "Ah, yes, I remember Daniel speakin' of you after joinin' my crew. He searched for you in England. Tell me, did you ever get to see 'im again before he was killed?"

"No."

"What a pity," Kelley said with fake sympathy.

Still gloating, he stepped over to the women's cell.

"Kate, are you ready to resume yer position among the crew?"

"Position as what? Your slave?" Kate demanded bitterly. "I'm tired of bein' a slave. I went to sea so I wouldn't have to be one."

"Whatever you want to call yourself is up to you," Kelley replied curtly. "But whether you want to or not, you are gonna work."

He ordered two of the pirates to bring her out. They opened the cell door and dragged her out with more roughness than was necessary. John did not like it one bit and came angrily to the door of his cell.

"Leave her alone," he demanded.

"Or what?" Kelley taunted. "I think you've forgotten where you are and the position you're in."

He chuckled evilly before turning his cruel gaze to Skye. "Well, Miss McHenry, here we are again. Now that you're back on my ship, what am I gonna do with you? You're a mighty hard worker; I'll give you that. That bein' the case, I think it would be beneficial to me to have you keep workin' until I have *other* plans for you."

Skye swallowed hard. Who knew what ideas formed in his evil mind?

Kelley ordered one of the pirates to take Skye out as well. This time Will came to the door of the other cell.

"Don't you harm her, Kelley," he warned with all seriousness.

Kelley turned to him, smirking. "Like John, you seem to be forgettin' who has the upper hand here." He walked to the door and stood face to face with Will, looking him over, a malicious plan formulating. "You look like a strong, hard worker yourself. Would you like to get outta that cell and work for me so you can keep an eye on Miss McHenry here?"

"Yes," Will answered without a moment's hesitation. He did not care what Kelley made him do or if Kelley realized he was only doing it to watch over Skye. All he wanted was to be near her, to make sure she was safe.

Kelley ordered the pirates to unlock the cell. As they were unlocking it, John spoke quickly and persuasively.

"Listen, Kelley, why don't you put the women back in their cell and let us three stronger men do the work?"

Kelley shook his head. "I like things the way I have 'em now. You two are stayin' where you are because I believe you're the ones who could cause me the most trouble, and I'm not gonna risk it. I'd rather have one man to keep an eye on, who I don't believe will attempt anythin' anyway for fear of somethin' happenin' to Miss McHenry, than to have to watch all three of you." He glanced at Will as he spoke, intending for the words to be a clear warning to him.

The pirates pulled Will from the cell and relocked the door and then forced him and the women up on deck. When they reached it, Kelley gave the three of them orders. Skye and Kate worked with or near each other for most of the day, and they found their work much the same as it had been before—monotonous and tiring, but not horribly exhausting.

But for Will, things were much different. Kelley gave him all of the hardest jobs around the ship—jobs that no one should have had to do alone or all in the same day. Skye and Kate were at least allowed brief pauses between the work, but it was not so for Will. Kelley kept on him, never giving him even a moment's rest, and Skye knew with great sorrow that he did it specifically to spite her.

Every time Kelley gave Will a new and harder job, he would look at Skye with a smirk to gauge her reaction. Skye tried not to let him see how much what he was doing to Will hurt her, knowing it would make Will's situation worse, but she could not keep her feelings completely hidden. Kelley seemed to catch every look of remorse and sadness that she sent Will's way.

Skye prayed fervently for the day's end to come quickly, though it seemed it would never arrive. But, when it finally did, the relief Skye had hoped for did not come with it.

She and Kate had just finished a chore when Kelley ordered his men, "Take Kate and Miss McHenry back down to their cell."

"What about him?" one of the pirates asked, nodding toward Will.

"He hasn't finished his work yet," Kelley declared.

Skye's heart sank, and she could barely hold in her sorrow. Will's work would take him, at the very least, another hour to finish, and she suspected that Kelley had given it to him as his last job on purpose. Skye could not comprehend how Kelley could be so cruel. Will had been worked since dawn with no food, no rests, and only enough water to keep him working. Now he would not even be allowed to quit with Skye and Kate.

A pirate took hold of Skye's arm to lead her below, but she yanked away from his hold. She had to do something.

"Let me help him finish," she said to Kelley.

But he just laughed. "Don't you want to go down and rest?"

"I want to help him," Skye replied in desperation.

Kelley laughed again and turned away, disregarding her words. The pirate grabbed Skye again and dragged her toward the stairs even as she struggled. Skye realized she had one last attempt, one other way she might convince Kelley to listen to her. Never had she intended to plead with him for anything, but Skye knew now she could not afford that luxury. Not at Will's expense.

"Captain Kelley . . . please," she called as they reached the hatchway that led below. "Let me help him."

The pirate dragging her stopped, and Kelley paused mid step, shocked by her choice of words. He turned and took a few steps closer.

"What did you say?" he asked, wanting to hear it again.

Skye forced herself to repeat the words. "Please, let me help him."

Kelley stared at her with a cruel expression, triumphant over the fact that he had finally driven her to plead with him.

"All right, Miss McHenry. Go ahead."

Skye found herself shocked that he actually let her. Not willing to chance he would change his mind, she pulled herself away from the pirate and hurried over to Will, who had watched the exchange.

"You should have gone down with Kate," he told Skye when she reached him.

"I couldn't let you finish this alone," Skye replied, shaking her head. "Not after how hard Kelley has worked you all day."

She set to work helping him. After a moment, she peered at him, worry in her eyes, and asked, "Are you all right, Will?"

"Yes," he answered quickly, not returning her gaze.

Skye knew, because he would not look at her, that he was only saying it to set her mind at rest. She could easily see he had been worked almost to his limit. His strength was nearly gone, his arms and hands trembled slightly from the continuous and exhausting labor, his breathing was heavy, and sweat soaked his clothes. This had only been the first day. What would happen if Kelley continued to work Will like this during the rest of the trip to Malvado four days away? Skye couldn't bear the thought.

"Will, if Kelley gives you a choice tomorrow, you must choose not to work again," she pleaded with him.

But he shook his head stubbornly. "I have to know you're safe," Will insisted. "I can't sit down there all day not knowing where you are or what you're doing. That was the hardest part for me while trying to find you. I can't do that again."

"But can you do *this* again?" Skye didn't even want to think about it.

This time Will looked at her and answered earnestly. "Yes."

Skye didn't understand, but Will knew that he could keep on with the strength he was asking God to give him if he was certain Skye was not being harmed.

"I don't think things will continue to be this hard," Will reasoned after a moment. "Kelley can't keep finding jobs like this for me forever."

Skye knew he was right, but he would have to last until then.

Chapter Sixteen

The four days of sailing it took to reach Malvado felt like an eternity to Skye and the others. Endless hours dragged on torturously, and Skye found her hope crumbling. She knew she was wrong, but she could not help but hate Kelley for what he was doing. Trying so hard to banish these feelings, she only found them intensifying with each passing day.

After that first day, Kelley never again gave Will the choice between staying in his cell or working on deck, and he worked him from dawn until dark just as hard. Though Will had been right that Kelley would run out of exhausting jobs to give him, Kelley still went out of his way to make sure the jobs Will was given were the hardest available. In addition to those jobs, Kelley forced Will to bring him his supper every night. Skye believed it was so he could taunt Will with the smell and sight of the food since none of them were offered much to eat. Especially Will on account of how hard he worked.

Some of the most horrible times for Skye came when Will would make a mistake or Kelley, for whatever reason, would be displeased with his work. Skye saw Kelley hit and kick him several times. Will had a few cuts on his face and bruises to prove it. Each time it happened, Skye's heart would break, and it hurt worse than if Kelley had actually done it to her.

Despite how difficult it was, Skye was determined not to lose sight of the fact that it could have been even worse. Kelley had threatened to do far more to Will, having twice brought out his whip, but one thing always stopped him. Skye, who had once thought she would never plead with Kelley for anything, now found herself pleading with him regularly. For some reason, her pleas had stopped him, but after the first day or two, it backfired on her. Kelley purposely mistreated Will just to hear Skye plead with him to stop. He loved hearing the once stubborn and defiant daughter of Daniel McHenry begging him not to do something.

Every night before she fell into a fitful sleep, Skye would sit and beg God to help them. She kept telling herself that He had a plan, but she could not help wondering what it could possibly be. She remembered her father telling her that the trials they went through in life only made them stronger and that God did not let anything happen that they were not strong enough to face with His help. Skye wondered how much more He was going to allow to happen, for she did not know how much more she could bear. Still, though it became increasingly difficult, she kept on praying and trusting faithfully, the only things she knew she could do.

Finally, late in the afternoon, Kelley steered the *Finder* into the port of Malvado. Just before dropping anchor, Skye, Will, and Kate were taken to their cells. Kelley would not risk one of them escaping. Thankful just for the opportunity to rest, they nearly collapsed. John, however, nearly about to go out of his mind with being locked up day after day, stood at the side, peering out of a crack at the pirate city where they had anchored.

"Sure says a lot about a man when he stops here, don't it?" John remarked. "'Specially when he treats it as any normal stop anywhere else."

Skye looked at him. Rumors and tales about Malvado were all over the Caribbean. The port was used by only the most merciless and murderous pirates. Just the quick glance Skye had seen of the city before being brought below gave her a sense of how sinister it was. You would have to have either a lot of money or quite a reputation to make it in and out alive. Kelley's reputation was certainly not an issue.

"I wonder how long we're gonna be here," John murmured.

"I heard Kelley tell the men just to pick up the supplies they needed and then they'd set sail again," Kate told him.

"Seems to be in a hurry," John commented. "Wonder why."

Any answers they came up with were not good ones. Two hours passed as Kelley's crewmen loaded much-needed supplies onto the *Finder*. When at last the ship was full, Kelley gave the order to weigh anchor and leave port. Soon they were again out to sea. In the cells, no one heard from Kelley until later that evening when a pirate came down to release Will. It was time to serve Kelley his supper. He let Will out and then confused everyone when he unlocked the cell Skye was in.

"Captain wants you to help 'im," he told Skye.

Skye wondered what about tonight was so different from any other night, but she did not say a word as she walked out of the cell and followed Will to the ship's galley. There they found far more food prepared than usual. It would take two trays to get it all to Kelley's cabin. The cook handed one tray to Will and the other to Skye.

"Take 'em to the captain's cabin," he ordered gruffly.

Will led Skye out of the cabin and carefully on deck. Along the way, he warned her with a solemn look, "Be careful not to spill anything." He knew from experience how Kelley hated that. "If you do, give your tray to me."

Skye did not reply, but she knew if she spilled, she could never allow herself to let Will take the blame for it. They reached Kelley's cabin and found him waiting like a king at the head of his table, every bit as smug as he had been the last few days, if not more so.

Skye and Will carefully set the trays down and laid out Kelley's food before him. As her eyes beheld the food and the delicious, mouth-watering aroma reached her nose, Skye's stomach growled. She was relieved when Kelley did not seem to notice. The very last thing she needed was for him to start taunting them.

Skye and Will then backed away from the table and stood silent near the door as Kelley ate, so they would be available in case he wanted something. This was what he had instructed Will to do, and Skye expected that he wanted her to do the same.

A few minutes into the meal, Kelley looked at the two of them with great satisfaction.

"A very fine meal, don't ya think?" he asked with a grin.

At the cruel taunt, Skye gritted her teeth, anger rising inside of her. Kelley continued, "I'm glad you two could join me in my little celebration. After all, tomorrow is a day I've been quite lookin' forward to . . . "

He let the mysterious comment trail off, and Skye and Will glanced at each other, confused. What would happen the next day that Kelley had cause to celebrate? Whatever it was, Skye knew it could not be good, and she didn't dare ask him. When neither spoke, Kelley's eyes settled on Skye. "So, Miss McHenry, yer treasure, will I get it all in one trip or will I have to make two?"

Skye was taken by surprise. This was the first mention of her treasure since Kelley had captured them in Puerto Seguro. It frightened her—the way he spoke as though he already knew where it was. His talk of celebrating frightened her equally, for it meant that he was confident. However, talk of the treasure made the stubbornness and determination never to tell him where it was well up inside her once more. Staring at the floor, Skye pretended she had not heard him. Knowing full well that she had, Kelley asked another question.

"Is it mostly gold?"

Again, Skye refused to give him an answer. Kelley sighed and sat back in his chair with a look of annoyance. He stared at them for a moment and then nodded at Will.

"Come here," he ordered.

Will glanced at Skye, whose eyes widened in fear, and walked slowly over to Kelley. For a long second, Kelley did nothing, but then he whipped out a pistol and pointed it at Will's chest. Skye watched in horror, hardly daring to breathe for wondering what he was going to do.

Kelley fixed her with a stern gaze. "As you were sayin', Miss McHenry."

The icy tone to his voice told Skye if she did not answer immediately, Kelley would likely pull the trigger.

"You would need two trips and yes, it is mostly gold," Skye told him swiftly.

Kelley grinned scornfully, noticing her use of the word *would*, but it did not concern him. Without a word, he slipped the pistol back into his belt. He then called for the pirate who stood guard outside the cabin.

"Take Miss McHenry and Mr. James back to their cells for the night," he ordered. "We have a big day tomorrow." His evil grin sent chills tingling along Skye's spine.

"Aye, Captain," the pirate replied and led Skye and Will below deck.

Once they were locked in again and the pirate was gone, Matthew's gaze fell on them in concern. "Why did Kelley need both of you?"

"He had more food tonight than usual and needed both of us to carry it," Skye answered wearily. She sighed, preoccupied. "But I don't think that is the real reason. He's planning something."

"Like what?" John asked.

Skye shook her head. "I'm not sure, but he told Will and me that he was celebrating for tomorrow. Then he started asking me questions about the treasure. Not only did it come as a surprise because he hasn't mentioned it since Puerto Seguro, but he spoke as though he already knows where it is."

John looked around. "Is everyone thinkin' what I'm thinkin'?"

Skye sighed heavily again. "He's going to do something tomorrow that he believes will surely make me tell him where the treasure is."

154

John nodded and Skye put her head in her hands in distress. *We need You, God. Please help us*, she prayed desperately.

That night aboard the ship was a sleepless one for everyone. Everyone but Skye spent the hours discussing even the most impossible ways of escape, determined to get Skye away from Kelley. Instead of joining in the discussion, Skye prayed almost constantly for strength and, above all, the safety of everyone.

No one was prepared when dawn arrived. A sick feeling of dread hung heavily over them. As the sun began to rise in the sky, Will walked over to the bars between his cell and Skye's. When Skye looked at him, he promised, "Whatever Kelley intends to do today, I won't let him hurt you."

Skye knew he meant that no matter what he had to do, no matter what cost, he would try to stop Kelley. She walked over to him and shook her head, speaking in a desperate voice. "No, Will. Please, promise me you won't. He's already threatened to do terrible things to you, and if you interfere, I know he will do them. I couldn't bear to have that happen to you, especially when it's because of me that we're here. I'm the one with the information he wants."

Will stared at her troubled but beautiful face and remembered everything that John had told him that one night on the *Fortune*. No longer did he care who was there or who heard him.

"I love you, Skye," Will declared. "For as long as I can remember I have loved you, and I cannot, I will not, let Kelley hurt you."

Tears of joy as well as sorrow over what would happen trickled down Skye's face. Staring into his deep

155

brown eyes, Skye saw clearly the love he felt for her. Opening her mouth to tell him how much she had always loved him too, Skye's words were cut off by the sudden eruption of cruel, tormenting laughter. Startled, everyone turned to find Kelley standing near the cell with at least seven other pirates.

"Pardon my interruption," Kelley implored in a voice saturated with mockery and sarcasm. "A very touching speech, Mr. James. Yer words nearly had me in tears. Do you intend to make good on yer promise to Miss McHenry?"

"I'd do anything for her," Will told him with no hesitation in his voice.

"Includin' die for her, perhaps?"

"Yes," Will answered before the question had barely left Kelley's mouth.

Kelley eyed him with a smug look as if he knew something they did not. "You may just get your chance."

Fear ran like ice through Skye's blood as she wondered what those words meant. She could never bear to lose Will. He had been in her life and had been there for her longer than anyone else she knew or had known.

Kelley turned to the pirates, "Take 'em out and bind their hands."

The pirates unlocked the cells and walked in to do their captain's bidding.

"What are you intendin' to do with us, Kelley?" John asked.

"You'll see soon enough," Kelley answered with a smirk.

They forced everyone on deck. Skye realized then that they were no longer sailing. Looking out over the ships railing, she saw a tiny island sitting not far away, much smaller than the one she and Kate had been stranded on. The captive group looked at each other worriedly. What was Kelley planning?

"Load 'em into the boat," Kelley ordered.

They were forced into one of the *Finder's* longboats, and when they were all sitting, the pirates and Kelley climbed in with them. Taking up the oars, they rowed toward shore. Skye's heart hammered loudly as she cried out to God to save them. In too few minutes, they reached the beach. As they climbed out, John leaned closer to Matthew and murmured, "I'll bet he's gonna maroon us."

The thought made Skye immediately ill.

When the boat had emptied, everyone turned to Kelley, but instead of giving orders, he reached out and grabbed Will by the arm. Yanking him closer, the pirate captain pulled out his pistol and aimed it at Will's head.

Skye's heart leapt into her throat.

"Here's the deal, Miss McHenry," Kelley announced. "You are either gonna tell me everythin' I want to know in very short order or I'm gonna kill 'im. It's a simple choice. Keep in mind that he just told you he loved you and is willing to sacrifice anything, includin' his life, for you. It's time to see if you love him in return and if you're willing to sacrifice as well. Now, I'm gonna count to three and when I reach three, I swear I'm gonna pull this trigger. If you actually go so far as to let me do that, then I'm gonna shoot each one of the others one by one 'til it changes yer mind. If you are still unwilling to tell me, well then, I guess you truly never will, and I am gonna leave you on this island with yer worthless, unbroken promise and dead friends to keep you company."

That thought was too horrifying for Skye even to imagine.

Kelley continued. "So, is one promise worth four lives or even just the one of the man who's just professed his love for you? I guess it's time for all of us to find out the answer to that question. One . . ."

Skye stared at Kelley with tears streaming down her face, her whole being crying out with sorrow. She remembered the day she had made the promise to her father. She had been so sure that nothing could ever make her break it. But she looked at Will and remembered his words on the ship. They were the most wonderful words anyone had ever spoken to her. Kelley said *two* and Skye knew that there was not even a choice to be made.

"Stop!" she cried just before he was about to say *three.*

Kelley stared at her expectantly, but Skye kept her eyes on Will.

"I love you, Will. I always have and my promise could *never* be worth your life."

Kelley smiled in victory. "All right, Miss McHenry, where is it?"

Skye finally turned her eyes to him. If she told him where the treasure was, they had no guarantee that he would not just shoot Will or the rest of them anyway.

"I'll make a deal with you," she said.

Kelley shook his head. "No deals. It's either the treasure or I shoot 'im, plain and simple. Now where is it?" he growled.

Skye had no other choice. She sighed heavily, for breaking her promise still hurt her deeply. "It's on Isla de Gracia, a week's voyage east of here." The promise she had kept for eleven years was broken.

Kelley blinked in shock. "Isla de Gracia? Island of Grace?" He laughed a cruel, hard laugh. "It was that simple? I should have guessed it." Finally, he stopped laughing and asked, "Where on the island is the treasure?"

"In a cave," Skye answered.

"There's close to a hundred caves on Isla de Gracia, which one is it?"

"I can't remember."

Kelley's anger rose. "Listen, Miss McHenry, I can still shoot him."

"No don't, please!" Skye cried. "I truly cannot remember. If I were on Isla de Gracia, I could probably find it, but I honestly can't remember to just tell you where it is."

"You'd better find a way to start rememberin'," Kelley said threateningly.

In desperation, Skye tried to remember how to reach the cave, but after the years that had passed since she had been there, it was very difficult.

Her brow creased as she strained to think. "There is a sheltered bay on the south side of the island where we anchored. From there, I think we went north. It was one of the first caves we came to. The entrance is partly blocked by a huge tree." That was all Skye could remember, and she prayed that it would satisfy Kelley.

Kelley digested her words. "Sounds easy enough, but there's just one other thing. I've heard that dangerous pitfalls are hidden all over in those caves. Are there some in yours?"

Skye hesitated for a moment, which did not please Kelley. "I'm not in a patient mood," he snapped. "Is it yes or no?"

"Yes," Skye confessed. "There are."

"And can you tell me where they are?"

Skye shook her head. "No, my father never showed me all of them. He always carried me through the cave."

Finally, Kelley seemed satisfied. "Thank you, Miss McHenry. You have made me a very wealthy man. I shall be thinkin' of you when I'm spendin' the treasure."

"What are you going to do with us?" Skye wanted to know.

Kelley sent them all a cruel grin. "This island is yer new home."

"You're just going to leave us here to die, Kelley?" John asked.

"Precisely."

Kelley backed up toward the boat, but instead of releasing Will, he pulled him along.

"What are you doing with him?" Skye demanded, her voice trembling.

Kelley looked at her smugly. "I'm replacin' the crew member I'm losin'." He nodded at Kate. "Mr. James here is a harder worker anyway. Besides, I need someone to go first into that cave of yers. I'd hate to step into one of them pitfalls by accident."

"No, Kelley, please don't take him," Skye pleaded, her tears returning. She took a step toward Kelley.

"Stop right there, Miss McHenry," Kelley commanded, his voice turning to ice. "If you or one of yer friends takes one more step, I'll have no choice but to shoot him. Look at it this way. You really should be thankin' me right now. I'm givin' him a chance to live. How long do you really think you four'll survive on this island?"

He continued to pull Will toward the boat, and Skye restrained herself, though it was the hardest thing she

160

had ever done. Tears streamed uncontrollably down her cheeks, her eyes locked on Will's.

Kelley forced Will into the boat and climbed in after him as the pirates pushed off and rowed toward the *Finder*. Skye stood at water's edge, never taking her eyes off them, wondering if she would ever see Will again.

Will climbed back aboard the *Finder* behind Kelley.

"Welcome to yer new life, Mr. James. That is, if you survive our trip to Isla de Gracia." Kelley chuckled cruelly.

Will, however, hardly noticed him. Instead, he stared back at the island and could still make out Skye and the others on the beach. How he wanted to be there with them, not only to be away from Kelley, but so they could all die there together if that was what God intended. He hated the thought that he might be the only one to survive, if Kelley did not end up killing him. He finally turned to Kelley, determined to help them.

"Kelley, for once, do something right and don't leave them there to die. I don't care if you keep me, but don't do this to them," Will tried.

Kelley scoffed at his words. "I wouldn't be worryin' about them if I were you. Worry about makin' sure you do your work well. If I'm not satisfied, I promise you there will be severe consequences, and Miss McHenry isn't here to protect you this time." Kelley shoved Will into the hands of one of the pirates. "Get 'im to work."

Chapter Seventeen

S kye watched the *Finder* sail off until it was only a tiny speck on the horizon. When it had disappeared completely, she sank to her knees, all hope and strength gone. Putting her head in her hands, she sobbed miserably. Nearly everything she held dear was gone. Her promise was broken, Will had been taken, and she and the only ones she had left were abandoned to die on this island.

Eyes on Skye, Matthew struggled to get his hands untied so he could comfort her.

"Here, use this," Kate said.

Turning to her, Matthew watched Kate pull out a knife from her boot. Matthew held out his hands and Kate cut the rope. He took the knife to free Kate, but she shook her head.

"Skye first."

Matthew walked over to Skye and knelt beside her. "Skye," he said gently.

She glanced at him through her tears. Seeing the knife, she held out her bound hands. When the ropes were severed, she let her hands fall into her lap, little caring that her wrists had been rubbed raw from the rough rope. Matthew tossed the knife to John and Kate so they could free themselves.

He turned back to Skye and laid his hand on her shoulder, hoping to offer what little comfort he could. Skye looked out to sea, with tears still trickling down her cheeks, and prayed quietly, "Please, God, rescue us from this island and help us rescue Will. Don't let Kelley hurt him. Protect him, especially on Isla de Gracia. Please let me see him again."

Matthew stayed at her side and prayed silently as well.

Skye shook her head. "I should have told Kelley where the treasure was back in Puerto Seguro. Then none of this would have happened," she cried in despair.

"This is not your fault," Matthew insisted. "Whether you told him or not, Kelley would have killed us regardless. You did the only thing you could do, and I am proud of you."

Still, it made Skye feel no better about her decision to continually resist Kelley. She felt as though she had hastened their fates and put Will in a dreadful position. The thought of never seeing him again tore at her heart as she remembered hearing his voice say the words she had longed to hear from him. Fresh tears rolled hotly down her cheeks as her eyes squeezed shut on the pain of it.

Behind them, John walked up hesitantly. "We won't be able to find fresh water on this island so I was thinkin' that it'd be a good idea to get outta the sun."

Matthew nodded. "Skye, we should do as John said and get out of this sun."

Skye simply nodded and allowed Matthew to help her stand and guide her under the shade of the nearby palm trees. Once there, Kate looked at Matthew and John.

"We should get a fire goin' so that any passing ships will know we're here."

John glanced around. "We're gonna have to be sorta careful with what we burn. There ain't much here."

Kate agreed, but said, "Any fire is better than none."

The two of them turned to search the island for firewood. Not wanting for John and Kate to be the only ones expending energy, Matthew said to Skye, "I'm going to help them. You can stay here."

Skye shook her head, trying to snap herself out of the terrible shock and despair she was in.

"I want to help," she replied. "I need to help."

"Are you sure?"

"Yes. Someone finding us may be Will's only chance of being rescued," Skye told him, her voice wavering.

Matthew nodded in understanding, and they turned to catch up with John and Kate. They each gathered up armloads of dry driftwood that had been washed onto the island by storms. After a few minutes, Skye had just about as much as she could carry when she stepped around the side of a bush. She gasped upon seeing what lay at her feet and took a step back. John, who was the closest, hurried to her side.

"What is . . . oh."

By this time, Matthew and Kate had joined them. The four stood looking down at what Skye had found. A human skeleton.

"Looks like Kelley's used this island before," John said grimly.

Skye closed her eyes and shook her head, two tears escaping. "What a horrible man," she murmured. What was worse was that he had Will.

They turned away from the gruesome sight and returned to the beach. Not long and they had a fire burning. The four of them sat down in the shade to watch and pray for a ship to pass by. All was silent as they thought sorrowfully of Will, each wishing he or she could have taken his place. It hurt Skye unbearably to know that Kelley would be just as demanding of Will as ever, and she would no longer be able to protect him from Kelley's wrath.

The day passed with an agonizing slowness, and the sea remained empty. The sun beat down on the island, making everyone hot despite the shade. At midday, they broke open what coconuts they could, trying not to exert themselves too much. They shared the sweet liquid inside and it quenched their thirst, but it would not be enough to keep them alive for very long.

At last, the sun sank low on the horizon, relieving them of its scorching heat. They kept the fire burning well, knowing that it would be even easier to spot in the dark. Unfortunately, things were not in their favor. Skye had overheard Matthew ask John if many ships sailed in that area, and he had said there were few. Still, Skye had to keep telling herself that it did not matter how many ships sailed there, they were in God's hands, and if He wanted a ship to sail past the island, one would.

The sun sank into the watery horizon and the island grew dark. By now, Skye was exhausted. Her body and her mind were simply worn out. Matthew noticed her tiredness immediately and encouraged her to get some rest. Skye was reluctant, knowing sleep would not come easily, no matter how weary she was, but she did as he suggested and lay down. As she tried to sleep, she asked once again for God to save them and most of all to protect Will.

Morning arrived and Skye woke to the sound of the wind rustling the palm trees. Ordinarily it would have been a lovely sound, but she kept her eyes closed, dreading the thought of facing another terrible day of wondering what was happening to Will and whether or not they would escape their island prison. She tried to blot these thoughts out of her mind, but what came to her then were the words Will had spoken to her on the ship. They were the last words Skye had heard from him before Kelley had taken him from her. Skye squeezed her eyes shut even tighter and a warm tear trickled down from her eye and onto the ridge of her nose, but she did not bother to reach up and wipe it away.

"Please, God . . . " but the beginning of Skye's whispered prayer trailed off. Something had reached her hearing, but what was it? A shout? Could it really be? Opening her eyes, she sat straight up and looked to the sea. Her eyes widened and her mouth dropped open. A ship filled her sight and already a boat rowed toward shore. She looked at the others, who still slept soundly.

"Wake up!" Skye called excitedly. "It's a ship!"

Her words were enough to rouse them instantly. They sat up, looking stunned and overjoyed when their eyes beheld such a welcome sight.

"It can't be!" Kate exclaimed in wonder. But by her tone she was not referring only to the amazing fact there was a ship at all. Everyone looked at her questioningly.

"It's the *Half Moon*!" she told them, thrilled beyond telling.

Kate was the first to stand, and she ran headlong for the beach and the boat that had nearly reached shore.

"Thank You, God. Thank You so much," Skye breathed as she pushed to her feet. She and Matthew and John jogged after Kate.

At the water's edge, they waited anxiously. When the boat reached them, Skye looked over Kate's crewmen. Something about them reminded her of her father's crew. The first one out of the boat was a middle-aged African man. He grinned at Kate who threw her arms around him, laughing joyfully.

After a great hug, the man said, "It's mighty good to see you, Captain. If we'da known it was you stuck here, we'd've rowed a little faster."

Kate grinned. "It's wonderful to see you too, Riley."

The rest of the crewmen climbed out of the boat and greeted Kate merrily.

"I hafta admit, Captain, we were beginnin' to lose hope of ever findin' you," Riley confessed. "Kelley doesn't leave many clues behind. Still, we were never gonna give up."

Kate smiled again. "I saw you behind us once just after I was taken."

"Yes, that storm blew us off course." Riley shook his head ruefully. He glanced up and down the island's beach. "Kelley maroon you here?"

Kate nodded. "Yes, but it's a long story, and we have to get back to the ship. There's somethin' important we have to do."

"What would that be, Captain?" Riley wanted to know.

"We have to go after Kelley," Kate answered, surprising him and the other men. "He has a captive we must rescue."

Riley nodded. "Aye, Captain, whatever you say."

His response left John frowning at the memory of his own crew.

No one wasted any time getting into the boat, and as they rowed toward the ship, Riley remarked to Kate, "I see you've made new friends."

Kate nodded. John, of course, was already well known to Riley and the rest of the crew, but to Skye and Matthew she introduced Riley as her first mate, and to Riley and the rest she took great pleasure in introducing Skye and Matthew. Riley and the others were very pleased to meet them and seemed to have a very high regard for Skye's father.

"So who exactly are we needin' to rescue from Kelley?" Riley asked.

"A young man named William James. He's very close to Skye," Kate answered. "Kelley's keepin' 'im as a slave."

"Do you have any idea as to where Kelley's headed?"

Kate nodded. "We know exactly where he's going."

"Where?"

"Isla de Gracia."

Kate told them briefly what had happened in the past three weeks. At the end, Riley looked at Skye and promised, "Don't worry, Miss McHenry. You can count on us to do whatever we can to rescue Mr. James."

The rest of the crewmen backed him up

"Thank you," Skye replied, touched and incredibly thankful for their willingness to help Will.

Very shortly, they reached the *Half Moon* and climbed aboard. The rest of the crew gathered round joyously when they saw Kate. She greeted them all warmly and then Riley spoke.

"Listen up, men. I'm sure the captain will share her story with everyone soon, but we need to set sail. Kelley's taken a young man prisoner, and we need to save 'im."

"What's our course, Captain?" one of the men asked, not showing any hesitation about going after Kelley.

"Set course for Isla de Gracia and don't spare any canvas. We need the *Half Moon* to get us there as fast as she's able," Kate ordered.

"Aye, Captain," the men replied.

Immediately, they hurried to pull up anchor and unfurl all sails. Once they were on their way, Kate motioned for Skye to follow her to her cabin. Inside, they changed into new pairs of clothing since the ones they had been wearing were worn and filthy from working on the *Finder*.

When both were dressed, Kate opened a trunk and pulled out a sword and scabbard. She handed it to Skye.

"You won't need it 'til we reach Isla de Gracia, but you can practice with it in the meantime."

Skye smiled and took the sword. She slid it part of the way out of the scabbard and her eyes rested on the shining steel blade.

"Thank you, Kate," she said. Her eyes rose to meet her friend's as she continued in a slightly lower voice, "for everything."

Kate smiled gently in return. "You're welcome."

Once back on deck, they walked toward the helm where John and Matthew stood with Riley.

"Wind's dead astern, Captain," Riley reported. "She's carryin' every sail."

Kate nodded in approval. "Good."

They had not been on deck for long before the crew gathered, wanting to know what Kate had been through. Again, she recounted the tale, but in much more depth this time. When finally she had finished, she looked at one of the crewmen, a heavier set man who turned out to be the cook.

"Bailey, the four of us could use a good meal. Kelley isn't generous when it comes to feedin' his prisoners."

"Aye, Captain," Bailey replied. "I'll cook up the best."

He hurried below deck to the galley, and the rest of the men returned to their work. When they were gone, Kate turned her attention to Riley.

"It's a miracle you found us on that island," she said. "What were you doin' in this area?"

"We knew Kelley was around here," Riley told her.

"How?"

"We stopped in Puerto Seguro five days ago and talked to Abe Foley. He told us you had been there and that he saw Kelley show up not too long after you did. We learned what had happened to the *Fortune* and realized Kelley had likely captured you again. When we found there were no supplies, we figured Kelley was headed for Malvado so we sailed there."

"How did you get in and out alive?" Kate asked in disbelief.

Riley shrugged. "We told 'em we were friends of Kelley. We said we had somethin' real important to tell him and that he'd be angry if he learned we were hindered. It worked and after askin' around, we figured he came this way."

Kate and John were both amazed and could not imagine how it had been done, but Skye and Matthew knew with great thankfulness that God had made it possible for Riley and the others to make it in and out of Malvado and then to find the island.

An hour later, Bailey finished preparing the meal and brought it to Kate's cabin. Kate and John and Skye and Matthew took seats around the table, mouths watering at the sight of food. They dished up and ate heartily. Skye, however, did not find it as enjoyable as everyone else. She could not help but think of Will and that he would not be eating much of anything for the next several days. The thought put a knot in her stomach, and she ate little.

When everyone but Skye had eaten their fill, they left the cabin. Kate took over at the helm, very happy to resume her role as captain, and John and Matthew helped out with the crew. Skye, on the other hand, found little to be done, so she wandered up to the bow of the ship and stared off into the horizon towards Isla de Gracia. She did not know how long she stood alone, but a voice came from behind. She turned as John walked up beside her.

"Will give that to you?" he asked.

Skye frowned in confusion for a moment until she realized he spoke of her necklace. She had been fiddling with it.

"Yes," Skye answered. "How did you know?"

"Just guessed. I saw he had one too and since he was a blacksmith for a while, I figured he probably made 'em."

Skye nodded. She looked back out to sea with a mournful expression on her face. John watched her for a moment before speaking again.

"Don't worry, we'll rescue 'im," he said. "None of us are gonna let Kelley keep 'im."

A wide smile came to Skye's face. "Thank you, John."

John shook his head with a return smile. "There's no need to thank me." He paused. "In the meantime, you need to start eatin' more. There's no reason for you not to eat just 'cause Will ain't. Trust me—he'd want you to."

It surprised Skye that he had noticed her lack of appetite and understood the reason for it.

"I know."

Before either of them could speak again, Kate joined them.

Walking up to Skye, she held out a Bible. "I remembered what you told me on the *Finder*, and I thought you'd want this. I knew we had one stashed somewhere, and I had Riley find it for you."

A couple of tears sparkled in her eyes as she reached for it and a smile spread across her face.

"Thank you so much, Kate," she said, her voice thick with emotion. "This means a lot to me."

Kate smiled. "I also wanted to tell you that whenever you wanna be alone, feel free to use my cabin. It'll be yours now too while you're here."

With those words, she returned to the helm. John left as well knowing that Skye would want to read. After they were gone, Skye took up Kate's offer and went to her cabin. She sat down at the table and opened the Bible. It had been weeks since the last time she had read it. Flipping through the delicate pages, Skye read all of the verses that had always comforted her most during the difficult times of her life.

Chapter Eighteen

S kye raised the spyglass to get a better look at the tiny speck of land growing in the distance. Isla de Gracia. This was the first time she had laid eyes on it in eleven years, and it brought back a flood of memories. Still, Skye's mind centered more on Will than the memories of past visits to the island with her father. At last, after the seven days of sailing, they were so close to being able to rescue him. All they needed now was a plan. Skye lowered the spyglass and looked at Kate, who stood beside her.

"We should anchor on the west side of the island. Kelley won't know we're there if he's in the bay on the south side."

Kate nodded and went up to the helm to instruct Riley.

Another forty minutes passed before they reached the island and dropped anchor. By this time, the late afternoon sun had dipped low in the sky. Standing at the railing of the ship, Skye looked out at the dense jungle of trees and undergrowth on the island. Colorful, exotic birds sang from the treetops, and monkeys swung playfully from the vines and branches. Skye briefly remembered how the island had fascinated her when she

174

was little. She even remembered asking her father if they could catch one of the rainbow-colored birds for a pet.

Kate walked up beside her with Matthew, John, and Riley, and her memories vanished.

"What do you wanna do now?" Kate asked. The rescue plan had been left almost entirely to Skye since she was the only one who knew the island.

"We've already decided that we cannot go up against the *Finder*, and if we're going to stop Kelley, we have to do it on land. So, I was thinking that we should go to the cave tonight and wait there for Kelley to come in the morning. That way we can catch him by surprise," Skye reasoned.

"Excellent idea," John said, anxious to face Kelley.

Everyone nodded in approval of the plan.

"There's only one thing we should find out," Skye cautioned. "If Kelley made good time like we did, he must have arrived here late yesterday evening and gone ashore this morning. I think it would be wise for us to find out if anyone has stayed on the island. It doesn't seem likely, but we can't risk someone spotting us and alerting Kelley."

Kate agreed. "We'll take one of the boats to the bay and see what Kelley is up to." Turning to her men, she commanded, "Lower one of the boats."

A boat was lowered into the water, and the four of them and Riley climbed down into it.

"Keep a close watch for trouble," Kate warned the rest of her crew. "We probably won't be back 'til dark."

Rowing along the shore, they navigated their way around rocks and in and out of small bays toward the southern end of the island. An hour later, they reached a large cliff which jutted out like a sheer rock wall before them. In the rocks were carvings and paintings that could have been many hundreds of years old. Skye recognized it immediately.

"This is it," she said. "Kelley should be just on the other side of this cliff."

They rowed cautiously. When they reached the end of the cliff, they stopped, able to see the *Finder* anchored in the middle of the bay. Skye picked up a spyglass. It was too far to identify individuals on the ship, but still she searched for any sign of Will.

"They are pulling up one of the longboats," she reported. "I don't see any on shore. Surely, if someone were still on the island, Kelley would have left a boat. Everyone must be aboard."

Skye handed the spyglass to the others so they could look as well.

"It seems that everything is the way we want it," Kate said after she'd had a look. "We should hurry back to the *Half Moon* and prepare."

Skye nodded. As Matthew and Riley picked up the oars again, Skye stared at the *Finder* longingly as she thought about Will. Where was he and what was he doing? She could not help thinking of the possibility that he could be dead, that he might have stepped into one of the pitfalls on the island or had an accident during the voyage. Skye took a deep breath and prayed that God had protected him. How she wished for some way to know he was all right.

Night had fallen by the time they returned to the *Half Moon*. A few lanterns lit the ship but not many to avoid drawing attention. The moon shimmered like silver on the water, giving them nearly enough light to see by anyway. Skye and the others climbed aboard, and the crew gathered around them, eager to hear the report.

"All right, men," Kate said. "We're gonna arm ourselves for a fight and go ashore tonight. Skye will take us to the cave, and we'll wait there for Kelley. When he comes in the morning for the treasure, he's gonna find more than gold waitin' for 'im."

The men chuckled. They, like John, were anxious to face Kelley and his crew, especially after everything they had done to Kate and Skye. Everyone gathered below deck to arm themselves. Skye sharpened the sword Kate had given her to make sure it was not dull from the practice duels she had engaged in on the way to the island. Thinking back to them, Skye had to chuckle a little as she thought of the one she'd had with John during which Matthew had told her of the duel between John and Will in Tortuga. A sigh replaced the chuckles. Skye longed to have Will there laughing with her, instead of having to laugh alone.

Putting her focus back on the rescue plan, Skye fastened a small dagger to her belt and picked out another sword to give to Will when they freed him. Lastly, she picked up a pistol and loaded it as a last resort. As she finished, Matthew came up to her.

"Are you ready?" he asked.

"As ready as I'll ever be," Skye answered, pausing. "This is the first time I will have to fight someone. My father only taught me to use weapons to defend myself if I had to." She paused again. "Have you ever been in a fight, Matthew?"

He nodded. "Once. It was during the voyage from England. We were attacked by pirates."

Skye stood quiet for a moment before asking, "Did you kill anyone?"

Matthew nodded again slowly. "Yes, to protect myself and the others onboard."

Skye sighed. Could she do what needed to be done to protect someone? Matthew put his hand on her shoulder.

"Don't worry," he said. "God will help you know what to do."

Skye nodded, knowing this was true, and slipped the pistol into her belt.

Before long, everyone was armed and returned to deck. They lowered boats armed with extra weapons, lanterns, and rope into the water and climbed down. Before she joined them, Kate looked back at the four men she had chosen to stay with the ship.

"If you see any sign of the *Finder*, get out of here. You'd be no match for Kelley."

"Aye, Captain," they replied.

Kate climbed down to the boats, and they rowed toward the island. Reaching the beach, they pulled the boats onto shore and lit more lanterns. Kate held one out to Skye.

"Lead the way," she said.

Skye took the lantern and stepped into the jungle, hoping she could find the cave in the dark. With everyone following, Skye prayed, *Please guide me in the right direction.*

Stepping carefully, they made their way through the thick tangle of underbrush. Skye often looked up at the brightly-shining stars to make sure they were always headed in what she believed to be the right direction. A long hour and a half later, they came upon a clearing and stopped. Off to their right yawned the black mouth of a large cave. A tree rose up like a magnificent tower beside it.

"This has to be it," Skye told them.

She knew in daylight she would have recognized it better, but it was more difficult in the dark. Breaking away from the group, she walked over to the tree. Matthew, Kate, and John followed. Skye ran her hand along a bare spot on the tree's surface and a wistful smile came to her face.

"Yes, this is it." She took her hand away from the tree, revealing three sets of initials—hers, her father's, and Caleb's.

After a moment Kate asked, "What should we do now, Skye?"

Skye turned and studied the area. "The trees on either side of this clearing will provide good cover. Your men could hide there. The four of us could hide in the cave and stop Kelley before he goes inside."

Kate nodded and turned to her men.

"Split into two groups and hide yourselves on either side of this clearing. Riley, you'll be in charge of one group, and Bailey, you'll be in charge of the other. We've got all night ahead of us, so make yourselves comfortable, but set up watches just in case," Kate instructed. "And one other thing. Make sure you're well hidden and don't leave any signs that we've been here. I'll give you further orders later."

"Aye, Captain," Riley and Bailey replied.

The men split up and hid in the trees. Kate looked again to Skye, who stared into the cave.

"Do you wanna go in?" Kate asked.

Skye broke from her thoughts and looked at Kate. "Yes, I would like to."

"All right," Kate said. "I think we're all kind of anxious to see your treasure if you don't mind."

"No, I don't," Skye said. Before going into the cave, she picked up a sturdy stick from the ground. "We don't want to step in the wrong spot."

Matthew nodded and handed her a rope. "Tie this around yourself just in case. John and I will hold it."

Skye tied the rope around her waist and led the way into the cave. Using the stick, she poked into the layer of dirt that covered the cave floor to make sure they didn't step into any pitfalls that were hidden along the way. She was already fairly certain where to step, seeing that Kelley had already been there.

They had not gone far when Skye stopped. Just ahead, she could see a pitfall. The bamboo chutes that had once hidden it were freshly broken. Instantly, she thought of Will, and her heart skipped a beat.

"Please, no," Skye murmured, tears springing to her eyes.

Matthew and John carefully moved to the edge of the pit and held a lantern over it.

John shook his head. "It's too deep. We can't see anything."

He and Matthew went for an extra rope and tied it to the lantern, their movements hurried but marked with dread. Slowly, they lowered it into the pit. Skye's heart pounded loudly with fear at every foot it dropped.

"It's empty," Matthew breathed finally in relief.

Skye blew out a long sigh. *Thank You, God.*

They continued on. A few minutes later, they stopped again, this time in a large area at the back of the cave.

Matthew, John, and Kate stared in wonder at the sight set out before them. Chests and crates overflowing with gold and other treasures were stacked against each other, filling the area. The light from the lanterns caused the gold to reflect on the ceiling and walls and in the eyes of every awestruck face.

"This is *all* yours?" John asked in complete disbelief. In all the years he'd been a pirate, he'd never had or even seen this much treasure at one time.

"Yes, it is."

"I heard the treasure was big, but I had no idea it was *this* big."

"It is significant," Skye agreed.

John shook his head. "Can you imagine the look on Kelley's face when he walked in here?"

"No, but the face he's gonna make when he sees us will be even better," Kate replied.

John nodded, a smirk coming to his face. "That alone might be worth a good portion of this treasure."

A moment later, Skye said, "Let's head back and figure out the rest of our plan."

When they had reached the entrance, Kate asked, "How do you wanna let Kelley know we're here?"

Skye shook her head. "I wish I knew the best answer to that. Surely, he'll bring Will with him. If we just attack Kelley with no warning, Will could easily be killed. We need to try to free him from Kelley first, before any fighting starts."

Everyone saw the wisdom in that.

"How 'bout when Kelley arrives, the four of us come out and demand that he release Will," John suggested. "He'd be a fool to resist someone who had a gun aimed at him, let alone four."

Kate nodded. "And after we get Will, my men will come out, surrounding them, and we can try to convince Kelley and his crew to surrender to us. That way there may not even have to be a fight."

"I like that," Skye said.

"What if Kelley decides not to cooperate?" Matthew asked, wanting to have a plan for all scenarios.

"Well . . ." Kate thought about it for a brief moment. "Then I guess we'll just have to fight 'im."

"There is one important thing," Skye told them, determined. "I don't care if Kelley gets the treasure in the end. I just want to rescue Will and keep us all from getting killed."

Kate nodded. "I'll make sure my men know that his safety is the most important thing."

"Thank you."

Kate left the cave to give the new details to her men. When she returned, the four of them settled down just inside the cave to wait out the night. After a time, John looked at Skye with curiosity.

"What do you know about this island?" he inquired. "Who made all them pitfalls and why?"

"Years ago, this island was used by natives as a stronghold when they were attacked. They would hide in the caves and use the pitfalls to stop their enemies," Skye explained.

John nodded slowly. "So who gave it a name that means 'island of grace'?"

"I believe the Spanish must have named it, but I don't know why they named it what they did. I only know that when my father heard about it, he felt it would be the perfect place to hide our treasure."

182

"Why does the word 'grace' hold such great importance for you?"

"Because grace is God giving us things, like the gift of salvation, even though we don't deserve it," Skye told him. "But also, Grace was my mother's name, and it's my middle name."

John nodded. "Skylar Grace McHenry," he said, after thinking about it for a moment. "That has a nice ring to it."

Skye smiled. "Thank you."

The hours of the night passed slow and quiet with no sign of anyone. On occasion came the rustle of leaves from some nocturnal animal. Skye tried to sleep when she was not taking a turn on watch, but it wasn't easy. She worried about what would take place in the morning and spent more time praying than sleeping.

Dawn arrived hours later and everyone went on high alert. Kelley would not want to waste time and would likely come to the cave very soon. In silence, they all tuned their ears to the slightest sound. The sun crept a little higher. Suddenly the sound of crashing brush came closer and closer. Skye's heart pounded.

Chapter Nineteen

Skye peered through the branches of the tree beside the cave. When Kelley and his crew broke through the brush, Skye held her breath in anticipation as her eyes searched the men. Great relief flooded through her. Will was with them. How she wanted to just rush out and save him.

Skye studied him closely. He certainly appeared the part of one of Kelley's slaves. His clothes were torn and filthy, but Skye thanked God that he seemed uninjured.

Patiently, they waited. Skye pulled her pistol from her belt and silently pulled back the hammer. Matthew, John, and Kate did the same. One minute passed, then two. Skye prayed for God's protection over all of them and that their plan would be a success.

At last, Kelley came within a few feet of the cave's entrance, and Skye and her group stepped into the open. Kelley stopped in his tracks. His eyes opened wide, and he stared at them with an expression of complete and utter shock. A wide grin appeared on John's face. Amazed and beyond thankful to see them, Will could not have been happier. His eyes locked on Skye's, and they shared a sweet smile before Skye turned her attention back to

Kelley. The captain blinked and gave a slight shake of his head, still trying to get over his shock.

"Hello, Kelley." John couldn't resist getting the first words in. "Did ya miss us?"

"How?" Kelley asked finally. "How did you four get here?"

"God can do anything," Skye told him with great pleasure. "I trusted Him to save us and He did. Now we're here to save Will. Tell your men to release him."

Kelley glanced at the two pirates who stood guard over Will. Skye could see he searched frantically for a way to regain the upper hand in the situation. After a moment, Kelley grinned, trying to cover up his true emotions.

"I'll make a deal with you, Miss McHenry."

Skye shook her head, remembering when she had tried the same thing with him. "No deals, Kelley. You either let Will go or we'll take him from you."

Kelley laughed unkindly. "There's only the four of you. How do you plan to do that?"

"Well, we may die trying, but I'd worry about my own life if I were you," Skye warned.

"Are you gonna shoot me, Miss McHenry?" Kelley asked mockingly. "I don't think you could."

It was then that John spoke up again. "I wouldn't bet on that one, Kelley. After all, you have the man she loves and even I know how dangerous it is to come between two people in love. But even if she doesn't shoot, you have more than just her to worry about. I guarantee you that from this distance I can't miss."

Kelley was now at a bit of a loss. He knew full well that John would not hesitate to kill him, and he wasn't about to try something stupid and lose everything he had just gained, including his life. He stared at the four of them for a moment before looking back to Skye.

"What do you expect to do once I free 'im? It will still be the five of you against me an' my entire crew."

"Just let him go, Kelley," Skye ordered, giving Kelley no clue about the hidden men who surrounded him.

When Kelley said nothing, John tried to hurry him up.

"Time's gettin' short, Kelley," he prodded. He then added with a sarcastic smirk, "And I'm not in a patient mood."

Kelley glared at him before turning to Skye.

"All right, Miss McHenry, it seems I have no choice."

Kelley turned to the two pirates guarding Will and made a show of telling them to release him. However, he also gave a signal, which Skye and the others could not see, to another of his men. The pirate moved his hand stealthily towards his pistol.

Will walked away from his captors, unaware of the danger as well. He had just reached Skye when there came a shout.

"Look out!"

The warning came from Riley. Skye was the first to notice the pirate with the pistol. From the instinct of wanting to protect herself and her friends, Skye swung her pistol around in his direction and barely took aim before firing. The pirate cried out in pain when the bullet penetrated his arm.

Everything happened in rapid succession after that. Riley and the rest of Kate's crew burst from the trees, and the fight began. Skye pulled out her dagger and cut the ropes that bound Will's wrists before handing him the extra sword. With a quick look at each other, they joined the fight.

Despite their best efforts, as bloodthirsty and pitiless as Kelley and his men were, Skye and her friends found themselves embroiled in a vicious battle. Each one was occupied to within an inch of his life. As Skye fought one of the pirates, Kelley suddenly came up and pushed the pirate to the side.

"I'll take care of her," he growled.

The pirate stepped away, and Kelley made ready to unleash the full measure of his hatred. Skye took a deep breath and prepared herself for his attack, knowing it would be brutal. Everything her father had taught her would have to be used now.

Kelley's first attack was even more fierce than Skye had thought it would be. It caught her off guard, but she quickly recovered and anticipated more of the same. For several minutes, she parried attack after attack with great skill which only fueled Kelley's fury. Then, in one perilous instant, Skye failed to react fast enough, and Kelley's blade sliced deep into her right arm. Stunned, she retreated, groaning in pain, desperate to recover. As Kelley lunged to pursue her, she took her sword in her other hand, but she was not as skillful with her left. She rallied, but sensing victory, Kelley came up close and hit her hard, knocking her to the ground. He kicked her sword away and loomed over her, grinning with loathing and triumph. Though dazed, Skye tried to rise but fell back again, her eyes riveted on those of the man who was about to take her life.

"You didn't honestly think you could stop me, did you?" he sneered.

Kelley raised his sword to deliver a last killing blow and Skye's eyes searched poignantly for Will. She caught one last glimpse of him, engaged in his own desperate fight, closed her eyes tight, and braced herself. But Kelley's sword never came down. She opened her eyes again to find him standing utterly still. Someone held a pistol to his head, but she could not see who it was because Kelley blocked his face from view.

"Touch her again, Kelley, and I will pull this trigger."

Everything inside of Skye stilled and all the commotion around her vanished for a moment. She knew that voice. *No, it's impossible!*

"Step away from her and drop your sword," the man demanded.

Kelley obeyed and stepped away from Skye, bringing the other man into view. Skye's heart nearly stopped in her chest and tears sprang to her eyes.

"Father," she murmured in disbelief.

Daniel McHenry took in the sight of his daughter, getting his first real look at the beautiful young woman she had become in his long absence.

"Skye," he said her name gently, tears filling his own eyes.

Skye rose, feeling as if she were in a dream. She took a step forward and threw her arms around him, clinging to him almost afraid he would disappear again if she let go. It hardly seemed real. Tears streamed down from her eyes as Daniel held her gently all the while keeping a close watch on Kelley.

"How can this be?" Skye managed after a moment, looking up into his face. "You . . . you were hanged!"

"No," Daniel told her quietly. "I wasn't."

Skye's questioning was cut short by Kelley's cruel voice.

"Daniel McHenry," he said scornfully. "I shoulda known that you, of all people, would escape the noose."

"He wasn't the only one, Kelley."

Skye turned toward the voice. "Caleb!" she cried with a smile.

"So finally I get to see the two of you together again." Kelley's anger boiled. "The two men who were always plottin' behind my back."

"We weren't plotting, Kelley. We were planning what to do with the rest of our lives. We certainly weren't about to spend them on the *Finder*," Daniel shot back.

"Both of you left without my permission and you, Daniel, took a very valuable prisoner with you."

"Grace's father paid you, yet still you planned to kill her. I wasn't going to just stand by and let you do that."

"Because you fell in love with her?" Kelley spat.

"Yes, because I fell in love with her, but also because you had no reason to kill her."

"So, Daniel, what now?" Kelley wanted to know. "I s'pose you're gonna kill me."

"No. I'm going to take you back to Kingston to stand trial," Daniel informed him.

"You must know I'm not gonna come quietly. I've got a better idea. You get rid of your pistol, and I'll get rid of mine. We'll fight each other fairly, and if you win, I'll go wherever you want me to go. If I win, I get yer treasure, no one tries to stop me, and I'll even promise to leave yer daughter alone for good. Even that way, you'll be gainin' somethin'."

"Will you have your men surrender also if I win?" Daniel asked.

189

"Yes," Kelley answered. "I will have my men surrender."

Daniel thought it over for a moment. "All right, Kelley. Throw your pistol away."

Kelley pulled out his pistol and tossed it to the side. Daniel stared at him for a long, tense moment and then tossed his away as well.

"Father, don't," Skye pleaded. She could not lose him again, not now that he had miraculously returned to her.

"It's all right," Daniel assured her.

He looked at Caleb and motioned for him to take care of Skye. Caleb walked over to her.

"Come on, Skye," he urged.

A reluctant Skye let him lead her away from her father, but she kept her eyes glued to him as he and Kelley clashed into a vicious battle. While she observed the deadly exchange, Caleb tore a piece of cloth from his shirt and tied it around Skye's bleeding arm. Then, much as she wanted only to keep track of her father, Skye forced herself to take her eyes from him and pick up her sword. Her friends were still engaged in fighting Kelley's men, and she needed to help them. Caleb stayed close, just in case she needed help again, and whenever Skye had the opportunity, she looked to her father to see that he was all right. He was just as fine a swordsman as Kelley, if not better, but it only took one wrong move, as she had found out herself.

Will fought off Kelley's men as best he could, but it was growing ever more difficult due to his lack of strength. As he sidestepped to dodge a pirate's blow, he glanced again at the man he believed must be Skye's father. He didn't know how it was possible for Daniel McHenry to still be alive, but Will had witnessed the look on Skye's face when she had seen the man, and he knew it could be no one else.

None too soon, Will's fight ended. The pirate fell before him and his attention was again drawn to Kelley and the man he was dueling.

Daniel stepped back from Kelley to await his next attack. Kelley glared at him, hiding the realization that Daniel was far better than he had been expecting. Then, in a flash, he reached behind his back and pulled out a pistol he had hidden under his coat. It was exactly what he had planned, devious to the core. He pointed it at Daniel with a self-satisfied and victorious grin.

Seeing the treacherous move, Will knew he had to do something. For so many long years he had watched Skye long for her father. He could not let her lose him again. He hurtled himself toward Kelley. Save for the fact that Kelley was ever in the habit of gloating at the moment of his triumph, the gun would have been fired, but Will grabbed his arm and pushed it away just in time.

They struggled against each other as Kelley fought to regain control. Will tried to pry the pistol from the pirate's grip and keep it pointed away from himself and anyone else, but Kelley was too strong. The man twisted the gun around and fired. A deafening bang exploded. Searing pain spread through Will's chest, taking his breath away.

Skye jerked at the shot and spun around. In the terrible scene that played out before her eyes, Kelley knocked Will to his knees. Will held a hand to his chest, and Skye lifted her eyes to see the smoking pistol in Kelley's hand.

"No!" she screamed. Fear and horror filled her heart as she rushed to Will and dropped to her knees beside him. Kelley backed away as Daniel rushed to Will's side.

"Will!" Skye feared the worst.

Their eyes caught as Will looked at her, breathing heavily. They both looked down as he pulled his hand away from his chest. A bullet hole was torn through his waistcoat, but no blood. Skye stared at him in shock and confusion. He pulled back his shirt, revealing his necklace. The metal cross was badly bent, but it had stopped the bullet and saved his life, for he surely would have been killed otherwise.

"Thank You, God," Skye cried, overcome with relief and amazement at the miracle. She leaned over and hugged Will tightly. For a second time she'd had to endure thinking she had lost him.

Daniel was the first to get back to his feet. He glared at Kelley, who had nearly taken his life and the life of someone his daughter obviously cared a great deal about. Only a miracle from God had kept them both alive, and it made Daniel even more determined to take Kelley back to Kingston. He had hurt far too many people and would continue if he was not stopped for good.

Kelley, however, had different ideas. He backed away, intending to try to get back to the *Finder* with what was left of his crew.

"Goin' somewhere, Kelley?"

Kelley spun around to find John holding a pistol mere inches from his face. He knew now escape was hopeless.

"You've got me, John," he said with a grim smile. "You can finally take yer revenge on me for killin' Nathan."

Everyone seemed to stop and watch. John had his finger on the trigger, and they all expected him to shoot. He looked as if he was about to, but his expression changed slightly, and he only stared at Kelley.

"Aren't you gonna shoot me?" Kelley asked. "Or are you too much of a coward to exact yer revenge?"

"Well now, Kelley, maybe I've decided I ain't interested in revenge," John said mysteriously.

"Don't tell me yer friends here have started gettin' to ya," Kelley jeered.

John just shrugged. "Perhaps they have." He looked past Kelley to Daniel. "He's all yours, Captain McHenry, just so long as you make sure he don't escape the hangman like you did. There's rope just inside the cave to tie 'im up."

Daniel nodded and went to the cave for the rope. By this time, Kelley's entire crew had surrendered, seeing their captain defeated. Each pirate was tied up and the wounded were tended to as best as possible in the absence of medical supplies. Skye and the others were amazed and very thankful to find that none of Kate's crew had been killed, only injured—yet another example that God had been watching over them. Kelley was the only one who had suffered any losses.

After doing what he could to help everyone, Daniel walked over to Kelley with questions.

"Do you have any men still on the *Finder*?" he asked.

Kelley glared at him hatefully and refused to answer. Daniel finally turned away and went to Caleb.

"We need to get the wounded to the ship. Go back to the *Grace*. Take her to the bay and see if there's anyone aboard the *Finder*," Daniel instructed. "We'll wait on the beach."

Caleb nodded just as Kate joined them. "Captain McHenry, when you came, did you see my ship, the *Half Moon*?"

"Yes," Daniel answered. "I'm afraid we worried your crewmen when they first saw us, but once I explained who we were, they were very happy to welcome us."

Kate smiled and turned to Riley. "Take some of the men who are not injured and go back to the ship. Follow Captain McHenry to the bay," she ordered.

"Aye, Captain," Riley replied, beckoning to his fellow seamen.

Caleb, Riley, and several of Kate's crewmen left the group and headed back the way they had come the night before. When they were gone, Skye walked over to her father.

"You have the *Grace* back?"

Daniel smiled. "Yes, she's ours again."

Skye smiled happily and hugged him again. "I can't believe you're really here," she murmured.

But she had no time yet to ask him the questions that spun through her mind. They had to get everyone to the beach. It was difficult to move the wounded since they were shorthanded, but eventually everyone reached the edge of the trees by the beach where the *Finder* was anchored. Fearing there might still be men aboard, they did not go out into the open.

While they waited for the *Grace* and the *Half Moon*, Skye made her way to Will. She had barely had a chance to speak with him yet. They smiled at each other and hugged again, their hands linking together when they parted.

"Oh, Will, I'm so glad you're all right," Skye said with much emotion in her voice. "I have been so worried about you."

"I was worried about you too," Will confessed. "I prayed so hard that God had rescued you from that island."

"Your prayers were certainly answered. The morning after Kelley marooned us, I woke up to see Kate's ship. They already had a boat on its way to the island," Skye told him.

"It's a miracle," Will said.

"Yes, it is," Skye agreed. She paused, eyes running over his dear face. "I also prayed that God would keep you safe and that He wouldn't let Kelley hurt you."

"Your prayers were answered as well," Will said with a smile. "After the first day, Kelley became so focused on the treasure that he seemed to forget about me most of the time."

"I'm so glad," Skye said with great relief. "I was so afraid when I saw one of the pitfalls in the cave. Who stepped in it?"

"I did," Will said, surprising her, "but I caught the edge and after Kelley and his men had their laugh they pulled me out."

Skye shook her head at how close he had come to dying and squeezed his hands tight. "God took care of all of us."

"Yes, He did."

"I need to thank you, Will," Skye said earnestly as she looked into his eyes again. "My father told me that you saved his life. I don't know if I'll ever be able to thank you for that."

Will smiled. "After how much you've missed him all these years, I couldn't let you lose him again."

"What you did means more to me than I could ever begin to tell you, and I am so thankful that God protected you. I would never have been able to bear it if you had been killed."

For a moment, they just stared at each other, both thinking about how much they cared for the other. Then someone spotted the *Grace* and the *Half Moon*. Skye turned as the two ships sailed into the bay. She grinned widely at the sight of the *Grace,* the beautiful, magnificent ship that had once been her home. Though it was only a ship, she felt as though she was seeing an old friend again, and could not wait to go aboard.

Chapter Twenty

Caleb and the rest of Daniel's crew searched the *Finder* and found not one man still aboard. Once the ship was clear, he ordered the men to take the longboats to the shore.

On the beach, Skye and the others watched the boats lower from the *Grace*. Standing next to her father, Skye asked, "Do you have a new crew?"

"No, actually it's many of the old members," Daniel told her.

Skye grinned happily. "You found them all?"

Daniel smiled. "Most of them, yes. I got word to a few and they were able to gather the rest. They are all very anxious to see you."

When the boats reached shore, Skye saw many familiar faces. Those who knew her greeted her with warmth and gladness, but their greetings were kept short as everyone helped to load the wounded into the boats.

"We'll take your men to your ship, and I'll have my doctor help you care for them," Daniel told Kate.

Kate was very grateful. "Thank you, Captain McHenry."

Once Kate's wounded men were comfortable aboard the *Half Moon*, Kelley and his men were taken to the *Grace* and locked up. Skye and her friends took the last boat back to the ship. When Skye climbed aboard the *Grace*, the whole crew gathered round her. These men had always been like family to her, and Skye could not begin to tell them all how good it was to see them. They too could hardly express the height of their own joy. They were amazed at how the cute, spirited seven-year-old they had last seen so many years ago had become the lovely young woman standing before them now.

After Skye had greeted everyone and had given or received a special word, she worked her way to Matthew.

"Have you told him yet?" she asked anxiously.

"No," Matthew answered. "I haven't had a chance."

"Let's tell him now," Skye said with a grin.

Matthew nodded and followed Skye to where Daniel stood amidst his crew, happily watching the meetings. He smiled as they approached and Skye said, "Father, I'd like you to meet another very good friend of mine. He and Will always took care of me."

Daniel smiled. "I'm very pleased to meet you. You have my greatest thanks for helping my daughter." He paused, his brow creasing. "If you don't mind my saying so, you seem familiar to me. Could we, by any chance, have met before?"

Matthew smiled. "Yes, we have, a very long time ago."

Very intrigued now, Daniel asked curiously, "When was that?"

"When we were very young . . . before we were separated."

A look of shock spread over Daniel's face.

"Matthew?" he murmured in disbelief.

Matthew nodded and immediately Daniel reached to haul his brother into his arms.

"I thought you were dead," Daniel said, still unable to believe it. "I searched all over for you for weeks!"

"I guess it wasn't God's plan for us meet again until now," Matthew reasoned.

Daniel shook his head, stunned over what he had just learned.

"There is so much we have to talk about," he said finally, his mind reeling with all he wanted to know about his brother's life these many years.

"Yes, there is," Matthew agreed.

But, like Skye, they knew that any stories or explanations would have to wait until those who needed care were looked after. Skye wanted so badly to sit down and talk with her father, but she put that aside to help with the wounded. First, however, upon the request of Will, she had her own arm bandaged. She then insisted that he too be checked to make sure he was all right, but he would not until everyone else was treated since he had no apparent injuries.

Finally, all wounds were cleaned and bandaged. They were all very thankful to find that none were life-threatening and everyone in Kate's crew would recover. Will was the last one to be examined. When he was finished, he came to Skye, followed by the *Grace's* old doctor, Aaron.

"Don't worry, Skye, he'll be fine," Aaron told her with a smile, having noticed her concern for the young man. "He'll be quite sore for a few days. If it were not a miracle from God, I wouldn't know how he survived being shot that way, but all he needs now is some good food and plenty of rest."

"Thank you, Aaron," Skye replied, her relief complete.

"Speaking of food," Daniel began, "I had Corey cook up enough for everyone."

In a short time, all who were able gathered below deck on the *Grace* around several tables. Daniel offered a prayer of thanks to God for His protection and everything He had done for them, and then they began the meal. It was the most joyful meal that Skye had been a part of in years. How thankful she was to eat it with the people she loved so much.

After eating, Will went to the crew's quarters to get some of the sleep he so desperately needed. When he had gone, the time had finally come for Skye to speak with her father. Together they went down to his beautiful captain's cabin. Just inside, Daniel gazed at her with a smile and shook his head.

"I can't believe how long it has been and how you've grown," he remarked. "It's truly amazing. You're the same age as your mother was when I met her, and you look just like her."

Skye smiled at that thought, and they took a seat at the table.

Filled with curiosity, Skye was quick to begin the conversation. "How did you and Caleb ever escape before they hanged you?"

"There was a young soldier at the fort. He had secretly admired us for the work we did and was quite upset to see us hang. Just before dawn, he made up his mind to help us escape."

In her heart, Skye thanked God for this intervention. She frowned a little then. "But how did I never hear about it?"

"The governor wanted it kept a secret. If other pirates had heard we escaped, they would have been encouraged to keep robbing people without the fear of consequences."

Skye understood, but frowned deeper.

"Why didn't you come for me?" She was confused and perhaps a little hurt too.

Daniel sighed heavily under the weight of that question. "Believe me, Skye, leaving you was the hardest thing I've ever done, and if I had known you were in that orphanage I would never have left you there. I thought your grandfather would take you in and you'd be safe."

"Where were you these past eleven years?"

"Caleb and I made our way to England hoping to gain an audience with the king to ask for a pardon so we would not have to be on the run for the rest of our lives. I didn't want you to have that kind of life."

"Did you speak with him?"

"Yes, and he lifted our death sentence, but we spent ten years in the prison there. When we were released, we spent the last year contacting the crew and gathering the money to buy the *Grace* so we could come back. I thought about you every day, Skye, and wanted nothing more than to see you again."

A couple of tears trickled down Skye's face. "I missed you so much."

Daniel stood up and took her in his arms.

"I know. I'm so sorry I didn't come for you," he told her, struck with guilt over what he had done.

"I understand," Skye said. "God had a plan when He let me go to the orphanage, and now He gave you back to me."

Daniel smiled and nodded, but then his face became serious. "Skye, I never meant for you to think I was dead all these years. I did write to you when I could."

Skye was stunned. "You did?"

"Yes, but I found out after I was freed that the jailer never sent the letters," Daniel told her with great regret. "The ones I sent after that must have been lost. I am so sorry you never got them."

Skye took a deep breath, wondering what it would have been like had she known he was alive instead of believing him dead. After a brief moment, she put that thought aside and asked, "What ever made you come here to Isla de Gracia?"

"I knew that Kelley had kidnapped you and that he was after the treasure. I didn't know what else to do but pray that you had told him where it was and would be here when I came."

"But how did you know Kelley had kidnapped me?"

"We stopped in Kingston, and I went to your grandfather's because I thought that was where you'd be. He told me what happened."

Skye nodded hesitantly at the mention of her grandfather, and her father continued.

"He also told me other things."

Skye's heart thumped loudly. "What things?"

"That he had always ignored you and treated you terribly. He told me he was very sorry and wished for you to know that. A couple of days after you were taken, he had ships sent out looking for you."

"He did?" Skye murmured, more tears falling from her eyes.

Daniel nodded. "He said you were a very special young woman, but that he had never acknowledged it and regrets that he didn't."

Skye was overcome with emotion. The thought of her grandfather saying such things filled her with indescribable joy.

After she had gained control of her tears and emotions, her father asked her to tell him her story. First, she poured out all about her life in the orphanage and how she had met Will and Matthew. Then she began the long tale of her whole ordeal with Kelley. Daniel was very pained to hear everything his daughter had been through. He was also very proud of her. She had endured more than many people ever could and had trusted God through it all.

"I'm so sorry all this has happened to you," Daniel told her when she finally finished, "but I am also very proud of you, Skye, and I know God is too. I'm so blessed to have you as my daughter."

Skye hugged him tightly. "And I'm blessed to have you as my father."

Daniel smiled. After a moment, he told her, "I have something for you."

He took a small wooden box from a cabinet which he gave to Skye. She opened it and grinned. The box contained everything that had been hers in the orphanage, including her Bible and the portrait of her mother.

"Thank you," Skye told him. "It has been so long since I've seen these things."

The rest of the day passed peacefully, something that Skye had not experienced in a very long time. When Will awakened later that afternoon, Skye told him her father's story. She also told it to Kate and John, who were curious as well. Daniel spent a long time in conversation with Matthew, having their whole lifetimes to talk about.

While they were talking, Skye spent time with the crew, right at home among them again.

Late that evening, once everyone had eaten supper and Skye was preparing to go to sleep, she went to her father's cabin and they read the Bible together, just as they always had when she was a child. Skye was so happy and could not stop thanking God for what He had done for her.

When they finished, Skye rose from her father's table.

"Good night, Father," she said with a smile.

"Good night, Skye. I love you so much."

"I love you too."

She left the cabin, taking her little Bible with her. She sought out Will, Matthew, and Caleb to say good night before going down to the comfortable, quiet, little cabin that had always been her own. She set her Bible and her mother's portrait on the nightstand next to her bunk and crawled into bed.

Early the next morning, Skye quietly made her way to her father's cabin to read together again. A short time after they were finished reading, Corey brought breakfast to the cabin. Will and Matthew were invited to join Skye and Daniel, along with Caleb, Kate, and John. They had a wonderful time together, but a little later that morning, it came time to think about leaving Isla de Gracia. Skye and Daniel met with John and Kate on the quarterdeck near the wheel and Daniel gave the two pirates a smile.

"I want to thank both of you for helping my daughter," he said sincerely. "To try to repay what you have done, Skye, Caleb, and I have decided to give each of you a large portion of our treasure."

John and Kate both insisted they had been happy to help Skye and needed no payment for what they had done, but Daniel insisted that they take it.

When her father finished speaking, Skye smiled at John and added, "And, John, since you are actually the one who stopped Kelley from escaping, and because he burned your ship, we have also decided to give you the *Finder*."

John's eyes widened. "You're givin' me the *Finder*?"

Skye nodded. "Yes, she's yours."

John grinned. No ship he had ever owned could compare to the *Finder*. "Don't worry, you ain't gonna regret that decision. The *Finder's* gonna have a new reputation."

Skye returned his grin. "Good."

Daniel then instructed Caleb and several crewmen to go back ashore and bring the treasure to the ships. It took many trips and a few hours, but finally, all of the treasure was split between the *Grace*, the *Half Moon*, and the *Finder*. Skye could not help but laugh as she listened to John talk about what he was going to do as the new captain of the *Finder* and what he would do with the treasure. He sounded like a kid on Christmas.

It was then time for the hard part, saying goodbye. Skye knew the chances of seeing Kate and John again were very slim, and she would miss them terribly.

"So, Kate, what are you going to do now?" Skye asked as the two of them stood at the *Grace's* railing just before Kate went to board the *Half Moon*.

Kate shrugged. "I'm gonna sail with John to the next port 'cause he'll need half of my crew to sail the *Finder* 'til

205

he gets one of his own. I can only imagine what he's gonna tell people when they ask him how he got the *Finder*, and I bet it'll be pretty entertainin'."

Skye laughed and Kate continued, "I'm not sure what I'll do after that."

"Well, I want to thank you, Kate, for everything you did for me," Skye said. "I don't know what I would have done without you. Even if we never see each other again, you will always be my friend."

Kate smiled. "And you will always be my friend. Also, I really should thank you as well. You've taught me a lot and made me see some things. When we were all on the *Finder* it . . . amazed me that you and Will kept on trustin' God through everything Kelley was doin' to you. Most, I think, would have just given up. It proves there's somethin' behind what you believe."

"Yes, there is," Skye replied earnestly. "God deeply loves all of us and is always there to help us. We just need to believe and trust in Him. He can help us do or go through anything." She held something out to Kate. It was the Bible Kate had given her. "I wanted to give this back to you. I have mine now, and I thought you'd like to have this one back."

Kate took it and ran her hand over the cover. "Thank you." She paused. "I'll take a look at it."

Skye smiled in return, thinking of the letter she had tucked within the pages of the Bible. A letter containing verses and explanations of God's love and His way of salvation through faith alone in Christ. "Good."

Someone cleared their throat. Skye and Kate turned. John stepped up to them a little nervously, like he was embarrassed.

"You wouldn't happen to have another one of those lyin' around, would ya?" he asked.

Kate stared at him in surprise. Before they could answer, someone laid a hand on John's shoulder. He turned to find Matthew smiling at him. Matthew handed John a new leather Bible that he had been able to get from Daniel. It also contained a letter written from Matthew to John, saying much the same as Skye's.

"Thank you," John murmured, taking it. "And I'll . . ." he cleared his throat, "I will read it."

Matthew nodded, pleased, still smiling.

When they had said their final goodbyes, John and Kate left the *Grace*. The three ships sailed out of the bay and into open water. The *Half Moon* and *Finder* sailed south toward the nearest port, and the *Grace* sailed northwest toward Kingston and home.

Chapter Twenty-one

Skye gazed at her father, standing tall at the *Grace's* helm. It was a sight she had believed she would never see again. Filled with wellbeing, she turned and joined Will and Matthew.

"I'm curious, Matthew. How did you finally get through to John?" she asked.

Matthew smiled. "The days we were locked up on the *Finder* produced some very good discussions, including one about revenge, and that's why he didn't kill Kelley. Also, he said much the same to me as Kate said to you regarding what you and Will endured, so I believe that influenced him a great deal as well."

"God used our suffering to get the attention of two people," Skye said, sharing a smile with Will.

"I think it will be more than two," Matthew suggested. "If John and Kate get saved, I'm sure they'll share their faith with their crews."

Skye agreed. She was so happy. What they had been through no longer seemed so horrible in light of the good it had brought about.

That night as the sun sank toward the horizon, Skye stood at the bow of the ship, watching the sunset. She smiled when her father walked up beside her. For a long moment, neither said anything as they admired one of God's great beauties.

When Daniel finally spoke, he surprised Skye. "Once I picked you up from Kingston, I was planning to go back to England. There's a nice house for us there and jobs as shipbuilders for me and Caleb."

Skye's face fell, wondering if he still planned to go back. "In England?" she asked, not knowing how else to reply.

Daniel saw her face and heard the sadness in her voice. But with a smile, he answered, "Yes. Either that or we could stay in Kingston. There aren't any big shops there for you to buy all the latest and fanciest dresses, but I guess if that doesn't bother you . . . "

Skye laughed. "Me, wear fancy dresses? You could hardly get me to wear a simple dress when I was a child. I wear dresses now, but simple is perfectly fine for me."

Daniel laughed as well. "I didn't think that would change your mind."

Skye shook her head and then turned serious again. "Were you really planning to move to England?"

"I was until I met Will and found that Matthew was here," Daniel told her. "After how long you've known them and how dear they are to you, I wouldn't make you leave now."

Skye smiled as her mind served up a few memories. "I don't know what I would have done without them."

"Especially Will," Daniel hinted with a grin.

Skye sighed and glanced at him. "You're not going to start teasing me now, are you?"

Daniel laughed again. "No. But how do you know I was teasing? Maybe I was serious."

"Matthew told you about us didn't he?"

Daniel shrugged. "Well, yes, but not before someone else hinted at it."

"Who?" Skye asked with a frown. The only other people who had heard her and Will declare their love for each other were Kate and John, and Kelley and a couple of his crew. Kelley was too angry to even speak with Daniel, and his crew followed the same example. Skye really didn't think Kate would have said anything. "It was John, wasn't it?"

Daniel grinned. "Yes. It was."

Skye had to smile as well, as she contemplated how John might have done that. She waited for her father to say more. When he didn't, she pressed, "Well?"

Daniel looked at her. "Well, what?"

"Well, what do you think of what they told you?"

Daniel seemed to think about it for a moment. Then he smiled.

"I think that William James is a remarkable young man, and I couldn't ask for better for my daughter."

Skye smiled. "Thank you. It means a lot to hear you say that."

Daniel put his arm around her shoulders and held her close. "It is strange though, to have left you as my little girl and to come back now and see you as a woman in love."

Skye nodded. "I bet it is. I'm sorry you had to miss it."

"Well, I'm very happy for you, so that makes it all right."

They were silent again for a few minutes until someone came up behind them. Turning, they found that it was Will. A smile spread over Skye's face.

"I'm sorry if I'm interrupting," Will said.

"Not at all," Daniel replied with a smile. "Actually, I was just going to see Corey about supper anyway."

He said it in such a way that made Skye wonder if he was simply giving them some time alone. When she caught an almost imperceptible wink in his eye as he walked away, Skye knew that was exactly what he was doing. She smiled to herself as she turned once more to look at the sunset. Will did the same and after a long moment, Skye told him of her father's plans.

"My father intended for us to move back to England."

"England," Will repeated dejectedly, in much the same way Skye had.

"Yes, but he knows now that I would never leave Matthew or . . ." she trailed off, their eyes meeting, ". . . you."

For a space of time, they looked at each other without saying anything at all, and then Skye gazed out at the sunset again.

"Beautiful," she murmured to herself.

"Yes," Will echoed, a smile in his voice.

Skye could tell that his gaze was still on her. She turned to him with a smile.

"I meant the sunset."

He laughed lightly and nodded. "Yes, that is beautiful too . . . though, not as."

Skye could not help blushing a little at his words and the adoring look in his eyes. With a sense of satisfaction, they turned their eyes to the sky once again, and Skye felt Will take her hand gently in his. She laid her head on his shoulder and happiness engulfed her. God had put her through so many trials and had seemed to take away everything that was dear to her, but He'd given it all back, as well as much more. More even than she could ever have dreamed.

Five days passed with perfect sailing weather. Those five days aboard the *Grace* were the happiest Skye had ever lived.

Midday was upon them when the *Grace* sailed slowly into the Kingston port. Skye, Will, and Matthew stood at the bow, staring at the city that was their home. Much had been done to repair the damage to the fort and surrounding homes. How long ago it seemed since the night Kelley had attacked the city.

They anchored the ship at one of the docks and prepared to go ashore. Skye and Will were joined by Daniel, Matthew, and Caleb as they walked down the gangplank to the dock and toward the beach. Near the end, Skye spotted a familiar face—her grandfather. Even with what her father had told her about her grandfather's change of heart, Skye was still uneasy. When they reached him, they all came to a stop and no one said anything for a moment.

"Hello, Grandfather," Skye said finally. Using the term grandfather when speaking to him felt strange. She had not addressed him in this way since she was a tiny girl.

For the first time in years, Skye's grandfather smiled at her, and when he spoke, he seemed completely different. All the harshness and anger were gone.

"I'm so glad you're safe, Skye," he said, returning her greeting. All uneasiness left Skye, just to hear him say her name. Her grandfather then went right to his apology. "I'm sorry for the way I have treated you through the years. I never should have allowed you to be put in the orphanage."

Skye smiled and shook her head. "God had a purpose for me there, and it's all behind us now."

"Yes, I do hope it is," her grandfather agreed with a nod, thinking she was a remarkable young woman. He turned his eyes to Daniel. "Until you find a place to get settled, I want you all to come and stay with me." Looking at Will he invited, "You as well, Mr. James. I heard you have quit your job, and you'll need a place to stay until you secure another."

Both Will and Daniel thanked him for his generosity. Before anyone could say more, Skye's grandfather insisted that everyone, including Daniel's crew, come to his house for dinner. Accepting the gracious invitation, Daniel told Skye, Will, and Matthew to go on ahead while he and Caleb sought out Lieutenant Avery to dispose of Kelley and his crew.

Skye could barely take everything in when her grandfather led them into his huge house. Though she had been there as a child, she never remembered it so large and magnificent. She also felt a bit out of place still wearing her worn breeches, shirt, and waistcoat, but for once, her grandfather made her quite comfortable.

Later that afternoon, after they had eaten and told Skye's grandfather about all that had happened, he looked at Skye with a smile.

"Skye, there are some things I want to give you," he said. He motioned to some of his servants, and a few moments later, several came in carrying three large trunks. "In these trunks are all of your mother's clothes and belongings that she had when she was your age. She would want you to have and use them, as do I."

Skye rose and went to the trunks. She opened them and gazed at her mother's beautiful things, awed that they were now hers. Smiling, eyes bright with tears, she went to her grandfather and did something that she never would have even been able to imagine herself doing not too long ago.

She gave him a hug, which he returned.

"Thank you," Skye told him.

ONE MONTH LATER

Skye stood in the beautiful living room of the new house her father had bought for them. It sat on a hill from which they could see the ocean. Daniel had instructed Skye to decorate to her liking, and it was a task she loved doing. She was nearly finished now and was just putting up some curtains she had made. Her grandfather had taken her shopping for the material, telling her to pick out whatever she liked, no matter the price.

As Skye was hanging the satiny, white curtains, she thought about the drastic change her life had taken from what it was a little over two months ago. She no longer had to work in the orphanage and had a real home to live in. Her friends' lives too had changed. In the time that they were gone, the people of Kingston had come to realize just how much in need they were of Matthew's services, especially with the repairing of the fort, and he had more than enough work to do. Along with the share of the treasure Daniel had given him, he surely would not be poor any longer. Matthew offered Will his old job as a blacksmith again, and he accepted it gladly, for he very much enjoyed it.

Skye broke from her thoughts when her father walked into the room.

"Now, there's something I never thought I'd see when you were young. My daughter sewing and putting up curtains in our house *while* wearing a dress," he said with a smile.

Skye smiled and glanced down at the beautiful, pale blue gown of her mother's that she wore.

"Well, I guess living at the orphanage did teach me a few good things."

Daniel walked over to her and kissed her on the forehead.

"You look lovely," he told her, "just like your mother."

"Thank you," Skye replied, her happiness very evident in her voice.

"Caleb and I were talking about going for a walk along the shore. Would you like to come?" Daniel asked.

Skye was quick to answer. "Yes, I'd love to if I could just finish with this first."

Daniel nodded and he took a seat on the sofa to watch her. A couple of minutes later, a knock came at the front door.

"I'll get it," Caleb called from the foyer. The door opened and he said, "Hello, Will, come in."

When Caleb led Will into the living room, Skye turned to him with a smile. She was thankful to notice that all traces of the days he had spent on the *Finder* were gone. All the cuts and bruises had disappeared, and he had gained back the weight he'd lost.

"Hello, Will," Skye said happily.

"Hello, Skye," he replied with a quietly earnest smile of his own. "You look beautiful in that dress."

Skye's eyes sparkled. "Thank you."

Will turned to her father, his face becoming serious. "Hello, Captain McHenry. I was wondering if I may ask you something."

"What is it, Will?" Daniel asked.

Will glanced at Skye briefly before answering. "I wanted to ask you for permission to court your daughter."

A smile sprang instantly to Skye's face. She cast her eyes toward her father, who appeared to be thinking it over, but Skye knew he was only prolonging the suspense. She was breathless as she waited for him to speak. Finally, he looked at her.

"Do you agree to this young man courting you?"

Skye grinned. "Yes."

Daniel looked back to Will with a smile. "Then, yes, you have my permission, and I wouldn't have chosen any other man but you to ask me for it."

Will smiled, his relief evident. "Thank you, Captain McHenry."

"You are most welcome and, because it is such a beautiful day, would you like to accompany my daughter on a walk we were planning to take?"

"I would love to," Will answered, his eyes going to Skye.

Together, the four of them left the house. Will took Skye's hand, holding it tenderly as they walked down the street behind Daniel and Caleb. When they reached the shore, Skye glanced toward the fort. Just two weeks ago, Kelley and all of his men had faced the consequences of their actions. No longer would they terrorize anyone at sea.

As they walked along the white, sun-warmed beach, past all the anchored ships and fishing boats, they happened to overhear a conversation between several sailors.

"My brother was there and said he saw 'em return all the goods that had been stolen. They must have gotten 'em from another pirate ship 'cause they ain't the ones what stole everything," one sailor said. "Looks like they've taken an example from Daniel McHenry."

"What two ships did you say they were?" another sailor asked.

"The *Half Moon* and the *Finder*, if you can believe that."

Skye and Will grinned at Daniel and Caleb.

"Well, it looks like they found the letters you and Matthew left them," Daniel told Skye.

Still smiling, Skye said joyfully, "Matthew is going to be so happy. We must go tell him."

They turned to walk back into the city. It amazed Skye to think in that moment just how wonderful her life had become. She had someone who loved her and whom she loved in return, she knew she would see Kate and John again whether it was on earth or in Heaven, her grandfather loved her, she had her father back, and she had a real home again and the family she had longed for. *Thank You, God, for the wonderful blessings You have given me . . .*